METEOR

COUNTDOWN TO
DESTRUCTION

J.D. MARTENS

EPIC Escape

An Imprint of EPIC Press
abdopublishing.com

Countdown to Destruction
Meteor: Book #5

Written by J.D. Martens

Copyright © 2018 by Abdo Consulting Group, Inc.

Published by EPIC Press™
PO Box 398166
Minneapolis, MN 55439

Printed in the United States of America.

Cover design by Candice Keimig
Images for cover art obtained from iStock
Edited by Amy Waeschle

Library of Congress Cataloging-in-Publication Data
Names: Martens, J.D., author.
Title: Countdown to destruction/ by J.D. Martens
Description: Minneapolis, MN : EPIC Press, 2018 | Series: The Meteor; #5
Summary: Robert Miller must work together with North Korean scientists to find a way
    to keep the larger comet fragment from hitting Earth. Major Winter joins him as his
    bodyguard, leaving Jeremy and Anna to fend for themselves at his mansion now that the
    Earth's temperature has returned to habitable levels.
Identifiers: LCCN 2017946139 | ISBN 9781680768312 (lib. bdg.)
    | ISBN 9781680768596 (ebook)
Subjects: LCSH: Adventure stories—Fiction. | End of the world—Fiction.
    | Natural disasters—Fiction. | Astronomy—Fiction | Young adult fiction.
Classification: DDC [FIC]—dc23
LC record available at http://lccn.loc.gov/2017946139

For Amy Waeschle, my editor,
without whom this story could not have been inked

1

NEXT STEPS

August 16, 2018
Somewhere in Northern Turkey

Karina and Dustin bumped at about fifty miles per hour along the uneven ground in the Israeli-government Cadillac Escalade. They could drive around four hundred and eighty miles between fuel stops. David Malka, Ben's father, hadn't spoken much to them, but Ben's mother Esther had been nice. Dustin tried to help out as much as he could, but there wasn't much to do. They were driving from the east coast of the Mediterranean, the great city of Tel Aviv, all the way to a city called Thessaloniki, where the Malkas had an airplane. Dustin thought how strange it all was; he and Karina had gone through so much to make it to safety in Tel Aviv, and now they were heading back to Greece by land to grab an airplane.

As they bumped along the road, Dustin thought about whether he could trust David and Esther. They seemed to only have taken him and Karina on to placate their son.

Dustin pushed his black hair out of his eyes. It had been a long time since he had cut his hair, and he felt skinny and depleted. He felt otherwise healthy and was surprised he hadn't gotten sick while cooped up deep under Tel Aviv. This wasn't the same for Karina, who had had a fever and a sore throat for about a week now. She was hiding it though, because they didn't want to give David any reason to drop them on the side of the road.

"Coming up on empty," David called out.

Dustin took that as his cue. They drove for another three miles, and then turned off the side of the road into a gas station. There was no one around. David pulled up toward the middle of the two filling areas and Dustin hopped out. He'd done this once before—the last time they needed to refuel the Escalade. He had a huge drill bit with an electric drill in his hand and walked over to one of the round metallic covers that led to the huge underground gas tanks. Dustin drilled a hole through it. Then another, right next to it, and another and another until he had created a small opening. He had to stop many times to let the drill cool down. There were many sparks, and the area between his thumb, and his pointer finger hurt from pressing all of his weight down on the drill. Finally, he created a large enough hole for his hand to fit through and turned the valve which opened the tank. Dustin slunk in the rubber hose, which was attached to a makeshift pump that David had made, and flicked the switch on.

Luckily they didn't have to repeat the process because this underground tank was not yet empty, so it filled their tank and all their gasoline canisters as well.

Once they got back in the car, David thanked Dustin.

"No problem!" Dustin replied enthusiastically.

"So, as we said, we can take you as far as Thessaloniki, and after that you two can go on your own."

"Sounds good, thank you, David," Karina responded.

Dustin shrugged over toward Ben, who looked unhappy.

Hopefully, they'll trust us enough to take us with them, Karina thought.

"So, Ben, you said you want to be a professional soccer player when you grow up?" Dustin asked.

"Yeah! I love football. My favorite player is Andrea Pirlo, the Italian midfielder."

"Wow, nice. He's an older one, right?"

"Yeah, I love watching his YouTube videos."

Esther looked to the backseat, saying, "One time we all went for Benny's birthday to New York City, and he got to see Pirlo play in real life! It was great! He had more fun going to that than seeing the Empire State Building or the Statue of Liberty!" Esther laughed warmly.

"But Mom, Pirlo wasn't even as good as he used to be. He was the best player in the world, or at least one of the best. He can really control the game, and it's really art what he does, and plus, the Statue of Liberty will be there forever."

"Not unless . . . " David spoke up.

Fortunately Dustin picked up the conversation quickly, despite the fact he knew almost nothing about soccer. "Yeah! So, you're going to play his position, middle field, as well?"

"Midfield," Ben corrected. "I hope so! If there even are soccer leagues after this whole end-of-the-world stuff . . . "

So, even little Ben didn't forget the end of the world, Dustin thought, admitting the little conversation with Ben did allow him a brief respite from their current situation.

They drove on in silence for a few hours, and Dustin began to notice their descent to a lower elevation.

. . .

"Jeremy, I need to talk to you."

Jeremy and Anna were in their small room under Major Winter's mansion. They were getting ready for bed, and Jeremy sat down at the foot of the bed, thinking his girlfriend was beautiful.

"What's up, my love?" Jeremy responded happily.

Anna looked up at the ceiling and then back down at Jeremy before saying, in a low voice:

"I'm pregnant."

Jeremy snorted in surprise. *No . . .* he thought. "What?" Jeremy asked.

"I'm—"

"No, no, I heard you. I don't know why I said, *what*."

"Oh."

"You're really pregnant?" Jeremy asked.

"Yes."

"Are you sure? Maybe there's some mistake."

"There's no mistake, Jer," Anna replied. "I'm one hundred percent sure."

"Oh," Jeremy answered.

Jeremy didn't know what to think. He sat on the edge of the bed, feeling the swirling mix of emotions wash over him. *End of the world, another mouth to feed, dangerous for Anna, insecurity for the baby, I'm too young, I can barely take care of myself* . . . The thoughts raced through his mind, not fixing on one but dashing past his mind's eye. Suddenly he flung his hands over his girlfriend's shoulders, hugging her tightly. They fell asleep holding each other, neither wanting to let go.

Jeremy woke up in a cold sweat a few hours later. Anna was sleeping next to him, holding her stomach with one hand. He didn't know if she always slept like that, but it reminded him of the baby inside his girlfriend. If the world didn't end, the baby would be born into a whole new world.

Jeremy got out of bed and changed his shirt to a dry one. He had been dreaming about running. It was a dark dream and his movements felt slow, like he was running in water. There were big beasts chasing him—fantastical beasts with the heads of lions but human torsos and big claw-feet. He woke up when they caught up to him, one of them biting him on the back.

Jeremy walked up the staircase to the ground floor of the mansion and over to one of the windows. The moon stared down at him, giving an eerie glow to the alien landscape before him. *Three and a half months . . .* Jeremy thought, referencing the date the comets were supposed to hit. The worst part about life after the first comet hit was the uncertainty.

The uncertainty wasn't just about the lack of laws, or that there were now probably tons of thieves and robbers ready to kill for food. There was uncertainty in the state and the boundaries between countries, although Jeremy was certain that the borders were obsolete. There was even uncertainty in the president's voice. President Chaplin had been president now for ten years; three more and she would break Franklin D. Roosevelt's record. She remained president because there was a security risk to the world, and apparently that was allowed, despite the constitutional amendment against third-term presidents.

The most recent government address two weeks prior had stated that going outside was deemed safe. Now, though, the government was silent. Presumably they were working on defeating the other comets, but everyone at the mansion was feeling restless—Anna included. The government was little help with food and policing, and the groups that had been trying to seize control—the Soldiers of God and the Union Anarchists—were silent. Their leaders were likely more preoccupied with surviving than guarding their territory.

It seemed like that was the major preoccupation of everyone around Jeremy now—surviving. It was all anyone had time for. Jeremy didn't know if his parents were alive. Presumably they were if they had made it to West Virginia, but he had no way of knowing. He also thought often about Dustin and Karina, but sadly he assumed they had perished in the months after the comet hit. It was dreadfully unlucky that they had been in Europe near the time of the comet's impact. He didn't even know if they'd gotten there safely. At least he knew Dr. Miller was still alive, and it pained him that he couldn't go with him to North Korea to try to save the world. Although perhaps it was good he wasn't invited to North Korea; it was no place for his pregnant girlfriend.

Jeremy looked up at the stars. He looked up often at night to see if he could spy the billionaire's Ark. Jeremy had been doing this for a long time. He remembered his high school physics teacher saying that he could see the International Space Station at night. Excited, he had gone outside, and sure enough, saw it darting across the sky. He had been surprised to notice how fast it moved. Unfortunately it'd been destroyed a few months prior by the debris from the first comet's impact. Now, however, he found it calming to look at the Ark, which would, at regular intervals, dart across the sky. Now, as he walked outside in the night, he watched it zoom by. He knew he was actually seeing the reflection of the sunlight on the Ark's solar panels, but it looked like a shooting star. He sighed and walked back inside, trying to keep his mind off Anna's pregnancy. *What are we going to do?* he wondered.

Jeremy walked back down to the tunnels below the mansion, past the bunkers of the Winter Militia, as they called themselves. *I wonder if they'll come up with a new name now that the major is gone*, he thought. Jeremy also considered that perhaps it was time for him and Anna to go, too. He trusted some of the men in the militia, but not all of them. There was one in particular, Elliot, whom Jeremy eyed cautiously. Jeremy found Elliot often looking over at Anna with hungry eyes, and even though Anna hadn't noticed, it made him uneasy. Perhaps their stay at the mansion had an expiration date.

Jeremy crept into the room, looked at Anna, kissed her good morning, and promptly fell asleep.

2

NORTH KOREA

August 17, 2018
Pyongyang, North Korea

Robert was amazed at how good Pyongyang looked in 2 A.I. Robert had started calling life before the knowledge of the comet B.I. (Before Information), and life after this date A.I. (After Information). In B.I. times, North Korea had been a dreary, unimpressive-looking country—one of the last communist dictatorships in the world. But in A.I., when much of the world had fallen to anarchy, Pyongyang stood tall.

The buildings were still erect—they looked communist and depressing, but they weren't destroyed! The roads didn't have giant potholes in them, and Robert didn't see abandoned cars on the side of the road. Even the mud and dust from the impact weren't noticeable. Robert thought all of this was very strange, especially after being in the United States, which had more or less descended into anarchy as soon as the people knew about the comet. From the looks of it, there was no anarchy present in North Korea. *Could it be the dictatorship saved this part of the world?* Robert asked himself. He wondered what the other dictatorships in the world looked like if North Korea had remained so intact after the comet.

Robert looked over at Major Winter, who nodded at him.

Robert stood in the small elevator with his own personal translator, a man named Mr. Yuan, plus Major Winter, and two North Korean State Security men—the North Korean version of the Secret Service. That awkward silence that comes with being in an elevator with strangers was about three times more awkward for Robert with this group of military men. He pursed his lips and scratched his back—the flask of vodka he had brought with him was almost empty.

Robert looked over toward Major Winter, who eyed the North Korean State Security men suspiciously. Mr. Yuan had told Robert that they would soon go to the laboratory to begin working, but first they'd go to their sleeping quarters. The United States' Secret Servicemen that had come with them were staying ten floors below them.

"Major Winter will stay next to me then, I expect?"

"If you would like," Mr. Yuan said, after looking and conferring with the State Security men.

The elevator ride continued up another five floors. When they reached the tenth floor, the elevator made a soft "bing" as it began to open. Robert was shown his new room, and what he saw made him gasp in amazement.

Instead of opening to a normal hotel hallway as he had expected, it opened to a grand dining room. There was a chandelier hanging over a large dining room and a large mirror on the wall to his right. On his left hanged a large portrait of Kim Ha Lee, looking regal in his dictatorial getup. As Robert walked through with his bags, he saw the back wall was a floor-to-ceiling window, overlooking the Taedong River and the skyline of Pyongyang. The television in the room was old, and the room felt aristocratic. Robert's bedroom had a four-post bed with ornate oriental designs carved into its posts. *This whole floor is for us, wow . . .* Robert thought.

"I'll take this one," Robert said to Major Winter.

Major Winter nodded, and walked across the living room to the opposite bedroom. Robert put his suitcases down on the ground and noticed Mr. Yuan standing beside him.

"So, you're going to be with me all the time, then?"

"Actually, I was just leaving. I will be back in an hour. In the closet you'll find the clothes you will be wearing for public appearances," Mr. Yuan answered.

"Public appearances? I don't need to do any public appearances, Mr. Yuan. With all due respect, we need to go to Dr. Kang right away. We have work to do."

Dr. Yuan didn't show any expression, but simply replied, "I am sorry, Dr. Miller. The Supreme Leader insists. I will see you in one hour. There are two State Security men outside your door, they will knock in one hour."

Mr. Yuan looked placidly at Robert, bowed, and walked briskly out of the room.

Robert swore under his breath and pulled out his computer, beginning to work on some new modeling software for the Vishnu spacecraft. They had less than four months before the impact of Comet 2—or Zeus, as Dr. Rhodes liked to call it.

The nuclear warheads from Vishnu, the spacecraft piloted by Dr. Rhodes, had made some progress in pushing Comet 2 out of the way. However, much more needed to be done, and this was what Robert had come to North Korea to figure out. Soon, Robert would know the full capabilities of North Korea's launch facility. The plane that Robert had come on had brought the nuclear warheads, which were actually not that large. Their housing and the material allowing them to safely travel through space was where the bulk of the construction lay, which was where North Korea would hopefully come in.

Robert's job was to integrate the bombs with the North Korean missiles, so they could be controlled and used by their systems. To make things even more difficult, President Chaplin had asked that he try to make sure the North Koreans didn't get any tips on how to build the bombs themselves—a task that Robert personally thought was ludicrous and unnecessary.

"I'm taking a nap, I'll be ready in an hour," Major Winter called from his room in the suite.

"Okay, Major."

The time went by quickly, and before he knew it, it was time for Robert to take a look at what he would be wearing.

"Oh, hell no," Robert muttered to himself.

In front of him was the same puke-green military suit that Kim Ha Lee and the rest of the North Korean oligarchy donned. Robert inspected his suit with visceral repulsion. In the other room, Major Winter also muttered a curse when he saw what was in his closet.

They don't expect us to wear this, do they? Robert thought. Robert thought about vocalizing this to his old military friend, but then he thought twice . . . *They probably have the rooms bugged . . . You're here to save the world, not to look good.* Robert remembered that story about the American college student who had been caught trying to smuggle a political propaganda poster back to the United States.

You're here to save the world, not to look good, Robert repeated to himself.

Robert put on the clothes while looking out the window toward Pyongyang. He could see the large square in the distance—Kim Il-Sung Square—was slowly filling with people, although he was too far away to see anything more than several orderly rows of heads.

"What do you think?"

Major Winter's voice traveled from the threshold of Robert's room, making him turn around. Major Winter was wearing the North Korean military green uniform. He walked uncomfortably in the suit, which looked to be about two sizes too small for him.

"I guess they don't normally make North Koreans in my size, which explains the tiny clothes they gave me."

Robert couldn't help but laugh. He even had a small American flag sewn onto his lapel, opposite the North Korean flag—*a symbol of unity maybe . . . ?* Robert thought.

"Dr. Miller, Major Winter?" Mr. Yuan called from the elevator door. "Are you ready for the announcement? We will brief you on the way. Since you have been living in the anarchy outside of the People's Republic of Korea I am sure you will need some catching up."

Robert and Major Winter looked at each other a bit confused and walked out toward the elevator, Robert holding his briefcase, containing all his work and his laptop. They both shifted uncomfortably in their new clothing and crossed the dining room to Mr. Yuan, who ushered them into the elevator. Two

State Security men, looking straight ahead, made the elevator an even tighter squeeze for Robert and Major Winter. *Well,* Robert thought, *it looks like North Korea isn't going to give us much time to be by ourselves . . .*

Robert and Major Winter were escorted into a black limousine. Once inside the car, Mr. Yuan started to explain a brief history of the past three years in North Korea. Robert looked annoyed at Mr. Yuan, thinking that it should be time to begin working. He spied the bar in the limousine and poured himself a drink of an amber-colored liquid, and as he took a taste, his eyes grew wide in surprise.

"So, as I was saying, when the comet—"

"I'm sorry, Mr. Yuan, is this Jack Daniels?"

Mr. Yuan looked confused, but answered, "Why yes, actually, it is. It is one of the Supreme Leader's pleasures to drink your American . . . how do you call it . . . bourbon?"

"That's it."

Robert motioned to Major Winter, who declined

his offer for a glass. Robert then turned to the State Security men.

"What about you guys? No . . . How about you, Mr. Yuan? No? Okay then."

"As I was saying," Mr. Yuan continued, "The Supreme Leader, in his infinite wisdom, knew that the comet was coming to Earth well before anyone else. We knew about the arrival of the first comet around six years earlier, and began planning for an impact accordingly. The Supreme Leader decided not to tell the people, thinking it would just cause fear and anarchy, and for some months the North Korean people remained ignorant of what was happening. However, once outside countries were overthrown by anarchy, including our neighboring China, the noble Kim Ha Lee built a massive wall around our entire country, and a speech was made about the evils of anarchy and our need to stand together as a people against both the comet and the anarchy around us.

"Life has been difficult since the comet hit, but the wall around our country helped us fend off the tsunami as well as the anarchist hordes around us. Food has been scarce, but thanks to the Supreme Leader we have persevered. We have learned that the United States has fallen, and in your wisdom, you managed to make a deal, turning to the side of the Great State, selling the United States' military secrets in exchange for North Korean citizenship."

Major Winter and Robert exchanged a look—and almost a laugh—each raising their eyebrows doubtfully. *That's not what we agreed to,* he thought, refilling his drink.

"We are going to be North Korean citizens?"

"Yes. We are going now to the Kim Il-Sung Square, where the Supreme Leader will introduce you to the people of Pyongyang and where you will accept the Medal of Allegiance, and listen to a speech by the Supreme Leader."

Robert thought for a moment, initially wanting to shout at the translator that this was ridiculous, and that Dr. Kang and he needed to start immediately on a plan to divert the comets. However, looking at the

State Security men staring coldly and robotically ahead made him rethink his strategy.

"Don't you think that maybe," he began cautiously, "it would be smart to begin working on the comet as soon as possible? I mean, without this publicity stunt?"

Mr. Yuan looked kindly to Robert, missing the point of his question entirely. "Oh yes, we will start right away. But Dr. Miller, public speaking is difficult for everyone. Do not worry, you won't be asked to speak to the people of North Korea. You'll just shake hands with the Supreme Leader—a great honor—and then I'll escort you to Dr. Kang and our scientific base in Pyongsong."

Robert took another drink and before long the limousine door opened and he walked out, shielding his eyes from the sunlight. He could hear a great thundering of applause, followed by the echoic reverberations of an amplified voice. The sound was large and full of importance.

The group walked down a black, carpeted path toward the back of a tall building. Major Winter was on his right side, Mr. Yuan in front, and the two State Security men walked behind him. Robert realized then that the Secret Service Agents that President Chaplin had given him as protection were not with them. He wondered if they were back at their hotel. They walked up three flights of stairs. The walls were filled with huge portraits of Kim Ha Lee and Kim Ha Lee's father and grandfather.

Robert walked left and right and left again, and then under an arch and through a door before arriving in a small room with a small door around more portraits of the royal family of North Korea. Robert could hear the muffled sounds of a speech occurring behind the door. Mr. Yuan looked back and said, "This is the alternate entrance to the main stage, and in sixty seconds we will walk out onto the podium. The Supreme Leader will introduce you. Don't worry—you won't be asked to say anything to the people now."

Robert thought he didn't mind giving the North Korean population a piece of his mind, but then considered that this might be the Jack Daniels making his head a little foggy, so he relaxed as the seconds wound down to walking out on the stage.

"Here we go," Mr. Yuan said, opening the door.

Instantly, a blast of air came toward them, accompanied by a booming voice screaming Korean. Robert adjusted to the racket and followed Mr. Yuan, who adopted an ear-to-ear smile. Robert followed suit, and looked to Major Winter, who kept a stoic look on his face.

They walked out to see an utterly spectacular view; a huge mass of several hundred thousand people stood in the square, clapping and shouting. Robert walked behind Mr. Yuan toward a podium where Kim Ha Lee spoke, with three Korean generals standing right next to him. He was smiling out at his people, and Robert took his place to Kim Ha Lee's right, beside Mr. Yuan. Robert stood there as Mr. Yuan ushered him encouragingly over to Kim Ha Lee and the podium. Robert took the hint and walked up to it, extending his hand. Kim Ha Lee shook hands with Robert and smiled regally over his people. Robert smiled out over the mass, too, which was well organized into neat long rows of subjects. Every person stood neatly in a line, wearing the same drab outfit. Since Kim Ha Lee stood at around five foot nine inches, Robert towered over him at six foot two. Robert felt awkward shaking the Supreme Leader's hand, but smiled at him and his people all the same. Then, Mr. Yuan ushered him back off the podium.

Robert stood on the stage and looked out over the crowd of people in amazement. *There are so many people,* he thought. It was amazing, and they even looked fairly healthy. *How had so many North Koreans survived the harsh high-temperature months?* Robert wondered. The isolationism and the dictatorship must have been an aid to their survival.

While Kim Ha Lee continued his speech, Robert had a look around. Surrounding the stage was a large building constructed to look Greco-Roman. Robert and the others on the stage stood in the middle between eight huge Corinthian columns, and the entire palatial complex seemed to be made of marble.

It looked very extravagant. Robert was so high above the masses listening to Kim Ha Lee that he couldn't see more than the first row of faces clearly. Those faces, however, looked up at the Supreme Leader with true love and happiness in their eyes, and food in their stomachs. Robert was surprised; he had expected sad faces and angry, starving expressions to be staring up at Kim Ha Lee.

When Kim Ha Lee finished speaking, the people in the crowd yelled a few phrases in unison—which Robert didn't understand—and then Kim Ha Lee stood tall and erect as everyone bowed to him. Robert noticed that to Kim Ha Lee's left—past the military generals—Dr. Kang stood with a squinting, stoic expression on his face. He did not look at Robert.

Kim Ha Lee then left the podium and walked down a path different from the one Robert and Major Winter had entered on. After him, the generals left, then Dr. Kang. Finally Mr. Yuan motioned for Robert to go back the way they had come.

As they ducked back into the limousine and headed

for the laboratory, Robert spoke up, asking, "Your country has survived the impact event amazingly, Mr. Yuan, I am impressed. Do you know of any other countries who have done so well?"

"North Korea is unlike any other nation in the world, Dr. Miller, and everywhere outside of our great state is in anarchy," Mr. Yuan replied, but then added, "But some communist countries are also doing decently. Russia is still in contact with us and has a good amount of people living in the tunnels under Moscow and several of the other large cities. China, as well, is using underground bunkers. Japan successfully relocated much of its people underground also. I have heard the Western countries are doing worse, is that correct?"

"Yes," Dr. Miller said to the annoyance of Major Winter. He continued, "I have to admit that the knowledge of the comet hitting the Earth was not received particularly well by the United States' population."

What an understatement, Robert thought.

3

A RUSSIAN DELICACY AND NORTH KOREAN MIGHT

August 19, 2018
Ark Spacecraft, Medium Earth Orbit

Janice fingered the flash drive in her right hand as she sat in the cafeteria with Alex Chekhov, her one friend on the ship. Janice had discovered that bunkers on Earth known as checkpoints had been placed strategically all over Earth for the billionaires to use once they returned to Earth. The flash drive had all the checkpoint locations on it, with the passwords of each. She wanted to give this information to the people still surviving on Earth. Janice wished she had some way to contact Jeremy and his friends with this information, but this was impossible.

What if they weren't alive? She had no way of

knowing. Janice finished her meal; she was a quick eater now, especially since switching exclusively to space food. She sat, drinking the required water allotment, while her brain tried to figure out how to get the information to Earth and maybe, by a miracle, to one of her friends.

There was one possibility. She knew that somehow the Ark spacecraft had the ability to communicate with Earth. She knew they had a line of communication because she had overheard Mr. Kaser talking to someone about the political situations of different nations "on the ground." That also meant that there were people feeding the billionaires information, or perhaps acting as moles or spies.

"You know," Alex said, looking in disgust at his tasteless food, "when I was young, my father used to make us a kind of food, it was called *tyurya*. He used to make us eat it to remind us about the poor times of our family, and about how many Russians ate only that for years to survive. I used to hate it so much, and I'd whine and cry whenever he said we were eating *tyurya*. Now, looking at this disgusting food, I find myself loving every memory of that taste of my past."

Janice watched as Alex sighed and washed down the rehydrated chicken with some water.

"Do you know anyone still down in Russia? Anyone that's still alive?" Janice asked.

"Maybe. Moscow put all their people underground, and from the temperature readings of the atmosphere, no one could have survived on the Earth's surface for that long. Ironically, they're probably enjoying *tyurya* right now."

"Did the government of Russia still have power by the time you left?"

"Oh yes, Putin would not let his country lose control. What little freedom most Russians had was gone by the time the anarchy in the United States happened. He even used it as a point to show Russians that they were stronger and more 'united' than the 'United' States."

Janice didn't say anything. She drank her water

in silence as she tried to think of a way to somehow communicate with Earth.

"Can I ask you something, Alex?"

"What's up?" Alex said. He'd picked up several slang phrases, and she smiled at this one.

"What exactly do you *do* on the computer for work all the time? I have been updating the lists for checkpoints and I do stuff that comes into my mailbox, but I know I'm not exactly a super-skilled programmer."

Alex frowned and thought for a moment.

"Well," he began, "I'm on the IT team for the ship. When there are bugs in the software for, say, oxygen regulation in the ship, I run through the lines and find what is causing a hiccup. We have been testing everything so it should run smoothly, but eventually little cancers do crop up in software."

"Right, I remember all my old cell phones beginning to lag."

"Part of that definitely could have been viruses or bad code eventually getting into your cell phone," Alex said, "but last week, I noticed—completely by accident—that the solar panels on our ship were pointed in just slightly the wrong direction. Solar panels work best when they are pointing directly at the Sun, so I performed my own calculations on a simple 3-D geometry problem, taking into consideration the rotation of the Earth, velocity of the Earth, our own velocity, et cetera, and corrected the solar panel orientation."

Alex smiled, and Janice frowned, looking out of the window. She could see they were going over the southern United States, and saw the familiar peninsula of Florida with the watershed of Galveston underneath her. Next came the big fallout of the Mississippi River in the area that used to be the raucous city of New Orleans. *Wait a minute . . .* she thought.

"Alex . . . The solar panels, they are moved around based on a program that you wrote, right? I thought they tracked the Sun automatically or something, like they knew all the time where it was."

"Well, they do know, because I entered it," he answered.

Janice's face brightened with a kind of "aha" moment, like she'd just remembered the location of something extremely important that she knew she'd lost.

"You're a genius, Alex!" she yelled, a little loudly, and promptly kissed him on the cheek.

"Thanks, but I don't really—" Alex began, his cheeks turning red.

But she was already gone, running back to the computer room, hoping and praying that Jeremy was still alive. *If you are, I've got a very big present for you.*

• • •

Robert looked out of the window of the limousine, still surprised by the sheer amount of people still living in North Korea. They looked at the limousine with interest as it drove through the streets of Pyongsong, the location of the launch facility.

"Impressive, isn't it?" Robert asked Major Winter.

Major Winter was also looking despondently out of a limousine window.

"Huh? Oh yeah, it is. Crazy to think they are still so organized, too."

Robert looked briefly over at Mr. Yuan, who was smiling proudly upon hearing the two discuss his country.

"We will get to the base in a few minutes," Mr. Yuan said.

It was heavily guarded, and about a half an hour north of the capital city of Pyongyang. There were walls all around the facility, and everything looked new—even the barbed wire on top of the eight-foot wall. When they reached a gate, two military officials came out of a small building and approached them. Robert noted they looked healthy and well fed, and wondered again about the civilians whom he'd seen at the speech. *Is everyone in North Korea this healthy?* Robert suddenly became very nervous, thinking that Major Winter did not have a valid passport—and come to think of it, he hadn't brought one either!

But Mr. Yuan's credentials were enough to have them pass without having to show the armed guards any passports. They went under a metal gate, and Robert began to shuffle through his papers and information he had for Dr. Kang.

The driver stopped in front of the door of a large communist-looking concrete building. He got out and opened the door for them. Robert walked into a hallway bustling with engineers and manual labor workers, who were busy moving parts and big hulks of metal back and forth down the white hallways. Robert felt like he was in some alternate future reality, a future where there was no comet, and never had been.

"Wow," Major Winter said.

"Indeed. Welcome to the Pyongsong Nuclear Facility," Mr. Yuan replied. "If you would follow me, please."

Never in a million years did I think I would be working at a nuclear facility in North Korea, Robert thought. Then his mind shifted quickly to the nukes they had brought with them on Air Force One, and as they walked to Dr. Kang's office he asked, "Mr. Yuan, what is happening to the nuclear warheads we brought?"

"I was told that all of your equipment on your plane is being taken to this facility to be stored until you and Dr. Kang move forward."

"Excellent."

They walked down several more hallways, which were less crowded than the main one, and ended up at a small nondescript door with Korean lettering on it.

"Here we are, the office of Dr. Kang." Mr. Yuan bowed, and knocked on the door.

A voice said something in Korean and Mr. Yuan looked back at Robert, smiled, and then opened the door. *This whole not speaking the same language thing is going to make working together very difficult*, Robert thought.

He walked into the room and Dr. Kang was busy at work on his computer. Mr. Yuan took the role of translator once again, standing in between the two scientists. Major Winter stood behind them, putting hands in his pockets and looked aimlessly around the room.

Dr. Kang spoke a few words in Korean, and Mr. Yuan translated: "Dr. Miller, it is nice to meet you in person."

"You as well, Dr. Kang," Robert answered, reaching out to shake Dr. Kang's hand, who took it awkwardly.

"Please," Mr. Yuan said, and indicated for Robert to set up his workstation at an adjacent desk.

Robert sat at the desk and quickly connected his laptop. He then pulled up a model on his screen, which showed different examples of what would be most likely to happen if the comets were not to be bombed, based on information from the Vishnu spaceship and Dr. Nia Rhodes's observations.

He turned the computer so Dr. Kang could see it. *Is he even going to understand this?* Robert wondered worriedly. After all, it wasn't even in Korean.

Robert vocalized this thought.

"Oh no, Dr. Miller, Dr. Kang does speak a little English, and he knows the scientific words and will understand the technical aspects. He is just not great with grammar and speaking."

"Great, neither am I," Robert joked. He began his explanation of the diagrams on his screen, making sure to take breaks every few sentences for Mr. Yuan to translate. "I believe we need to explode the nuclear weapons in between the two remaining fragments, due to the helical travel vectors of the two comet system. This also coincides with Comet 2's largest gaseous pocket. We will focus the nuclear explosions on Comet 2—the comet with extinction capabilities. However, as of now, we do not have the capability to effectively expel Comet 2 from the collision path with Earth."

At a break in Robert's speech, Mr. Yuan began translating Dr. Kang's response: "We must also take into consideration the distance between the two comets, which varies from close to far apart. A nuclear explosion would have much less impact if detonated when the comets are far apart. I have created a model for predicting this, and think it will be helpful. After all, the nuclear explosions work best close to the surface of the comet. How many more nuclear missiles do we need to reach this threshold of necessary energy to expel the comet?" Dr. Kang watched Robert listen to Mr. Yuan, waiting.

"We need at least six successful launches and hits by Interplanetary Missiles, or IMPs, launched from North Korea. That is not counting the three IMPs that are still on their way to Comet 2, and the six nuclear warheads that the Vishnu spacecraft can detonate."

"The Vishnu spacecraft?" Dr. Kang asked.

Robert then filled Dr. Kang in on Vishnu, Gerald Jan, and the eclectic Dr. Rhodes who was in charge of the ship. A small man to Dr. Kang's right—whom Robert had previously not even noticed—sat madly typing everything Robert said into a computer.

"Um, who is that?" Robert asked, surprised he had not noticed the man.

"I am Dr. Chan," the man said in a Chinese accent, looking up. "I am transcribing what you have said so I can translate it and give the other engineers some information about what exactly we will be doing."

"Okay," Robert replied.

Dr. Kang began speaking again, his hands clasped about each other, and Mr. Yuan translated: "And if any of the nuclear missiles traveling to the comet fail now, our strategy will fail. So, we need at least sixteen successful nuclear strikes on Comet 2 in order to successfully avoid an impact?"

"Yes," Robert answered, flicking through his notes. "That's correct." *I should at least learn how to say "yes" in Korean*, he thought.

"I see. I will now take you down to the manufacturing floor. Here, we will see one of the missiles that will carry the nuclear armament into space. This will give you the opportunity to begin integrating the bomb with our missile," Mr. Yuan translated. Robert had worked with a Korean translator once before when he'd worked with some South Korean scientists, and it always unnerved him how it seemed like the translators weren't telling him all that was being said—like they were leaving something out and only giving him a summary of the words. *Maybe Korean words are just longer,* he thought.

"Very well, Dr. Kang. Lead the way."

Dr. Kang packed up his things and Robert followed suit, and they all exited the small room. Dr. Chan and Mr. Yuan also followed Dr. Kang, who despite his short legs was a speedy walker. They hustled back into the large corridor and what looked like out of the building, as they were headed for the same big double doors they had entered. But just as they were about to reach the door, Dr. Kang walked right, opening a small side door, and the group walked through it. Robert and Major Winter had to duck to avoid hitting their heads on the doorway.

Robert walked into a gigantic manufacturing floor with a cacophony of stamping machines, pressing machines, large movable cranes, forklifts, indistinct yelling, huge assembly lines, conveyors, process control checks, and hundreds of Koreans. The flood of fluorescent lights, which were lined up every six feet on the tall ceiling, made Robert shield his eyes. As

Robert walked behind Dr. Kang inside the yellow-lined walkway, Major Winter came up beside him.

"Hey," the major whispered, "you won't need to give the other scientists information about how to make nukes, right? I mean, I'm just thinking it would be bad if they had our recipe for making nuclear weapons, if the world keeps on living."

Robert turned to Major Winter. "Anton, luckily I don't know how to make a nuclear weapon from scratch—I'm just here to make sure we can integrate the nukes to their missiles. I have no doubt they'll try to get that information from us at some point, though."

"We should make sure to sleep with one eye open," Major Winter replied.

4

FLIGHT

August 30, 2018
Ark Spacecraft, Medium Earth Orbit

It was a simple computer script to write, and Janice wrote it in just under three hours. Her plan was simple enough, even though it was a long shot. When Alex mentioned he wrote code to move the solar panels so they were directed toward the Sun, it had given her a far-flung, probably unsuccessful idea. But, it was an idea nonetheless, and one that just might work.

She remembered living in the mountains with Jeremy and his friends in Colorado: one night they were looking up at the stars, trying to find the comet.

"Oh, is that it?" Janice remembered Dustin asking.

"No," Jeremy replied, walking over to Dustin and

Janice. "The comet is still too far away to see with the naked eye. That's the International Space Station. We can see it because the light from the Sun is reflecting off its solar panels. If the solar panels weren't angled like that, we wouldn't be able to see it at all."

That's where Janice got her idea. *The solar panels!* Janice's script simply moved the solar panels back and forth as they went over Texas. Maybe Jeremy was there, maybe he wasn't. She could hope, though. It took a little 3-D modeling to figure out which way to move the panels, but Janice figured it out quickly enough. Her plan was to move the panels back and forth, directing the Sun's rays from the Ark toward the Houston area. The solar panels themselves moved back and forth, essentially making the Ark visible or invisible at night for anyone looking up at the sky. Janice wrote the script so that there would be two different lengths of time for which the Ark was visible to the ground, one short and one long.

Her plan was to give a signal in Morse code. First, for a few nights, she would simply have the light alternate in breaks of short and long which would spell out "Jeremy Genser." She figured that if Jeremy was down there, and he happened to look at the Ark, he might notice that the "on-off" visibility wasn't normal. He then might eventually realize that it could be a code. It was a long shot to say the least, but once he realized that the code was his name, he would know that someone from the Ark was trying to contact him. Then she would change the pattern to a message containing the coordinates of a checkpoint close to him, with the password.

Of course, there was a small possibility that she would get caught. Since she would be moving the solar panels of the Ark, they would no longer be in ideal alignment with the Sun, meaning some amount of the Ark's energy would be lost. This would happen over time, and surely the engineers would think of other reasons the energy was depleting. They also had a small nuclear reactor on board, so it wouldn't be life-threatening for Janice or her fellow Ark members.

Also, since everyone was required to "sign in" to

use a computer, Janice decided she would use Alex's login. Even if someone did notice there was something wrong, Alex would only notice that the solar panels weren't working as well as he'd thought, and perhaps recheck his code. In that case it would only be Alex who would identify his own mistake, and even if he did suspect her, Janice figured he would confront her first before going to Mr. Kaser.

The much more obvious issue with her plan was this: all of this hinged on Jeremy being alive, being in the Houston area, and looking up at the sky frequently. Jeremy also had no way of communicating that he'd seen the information, so Janice would just have to hope her plan worked. *It's not like I have a better idea anyway,* Janice thought.

Before she finished, she walked around the ship, looking for Alex. She had already checked the computer room and he wasn't there. *He's not here . . . Damn*, she thought. She wanted to make sure he wouldn't walk in on her executing her code.

Alex was not in the cafeteria either, and after

checking the exercise room, the zero-gravity part of the Ark, and even waiting outside the men's toilets next to both the cafeteria and Alex's bed, he was still nowhere to be found.

Janice peeked into the room where Alex slept, and saw an older gentleman changing his clothes next to his bed. The other bed—presumably Alex's—was unkempt and messy.

"Oh!" she yelped.

"Hello, miss." The man spoke, unabashed at his nakedness, in heavily accented Russian.

The man did not feel the need to pick up his towel, but calmly continued getting dressed while Janice stood uncomfortably by the door.

"Excuse me, you're Mr. Chekhov, aren't you?" Janice asked, trying not to look embarrassed while the naked old man in front of her combed his hair.

"*Da*," the man affirmed. "And you are?"

"Mr. Chekhov, I'm a friend of Alex's. I'm trying to find him. Do you know where he is?"

"The kitchen, I think. I don't know why he must always go to the kitchen."

Mr. Chekhov stood there contemplatively while Janice forced herself to keep her head up. She excused herself and made for the kitchen. *God, why are all old people so free with their bodies?* Janice thought, annoyed. She walked into the large kitchen, which was communal. It was a little ironic since most people on the Ark had never cooked for themselves. Sure, some of them made their own money, and thus remembered struggling to put food on the table, but those like Janice's father inherited money, and simply used it to make more money.

Once the space food was all eaten, they would need to turn to the grown vegetables and starches which were almost finished in the greenhouse section of the spacecraft. It was funny to think that soon people would have to start cooking for themselves, and this would especially be true once they returned to Earth.

For the sake of cleanliness, the galley was located in the artificial gravity sector of the ship. When Janice walked in she saw Alex reorganizing all the pots and pans. Confused, she stood there watching him, feeling like she was intruding. The pots and pans, like everything else on the Ark, used up as little space as possible, so there wasn't really much reorganizing Alex could do. All the same, he simply took out all of the pots, placed them on the counter, and moved them around, pretending to clean them, wash them, and dry them. The whole situation felt very intimate, which made Janice uncomfortable.

"Hi Alex," she said, momentarily forgetting why she had come to see him in the first place.

"Oh, hey, um," Alex started to speak, but looked around uncomfortably.

Neither spoke for a long minute.

"I didn't mean to bother you," Janice said, turning to leave.

Alex turned around, and spoke. "No, no, it's okay. When I was little—only around five or six years old—it was just me and my mother, in a little apartment in Moscow. My mother would work all night at a bar as a cocktail waitress, and when she would get home, she would make me breakfast. She would always say I had to do the dishes. 'I cooked—you do the dishes.' That's what she'd say. She would always make me do them and stand next to me, and even though I'd hate to wash them and put them away, it was the one time in my life when my mother and I would be able to talk. I haven't seen her in a long time . . . " Alex's voice drifted off.

"I'm sorry, Alex."

Alex looked up and smiled over at Janice while still holding a baking sheet.

"Don't worry," he said.

They stood there for a little while until Alex shook himself slightly. To Janice it looked like he had just shaken off bad feelings, letting them fall right to the floor.

"Well," Alex said a little more brightly, "I'm starving. I'm going to head to the cafeteria. Do you want to join me?"

"Thank you, Alex, but I have some work I need to do," Janice replied.

"Okay, sure. I'll see you later then."

Alex smiled at Janice and rubbed her shoulder with his hand as he walked by her. He exited the kitchen and walked left toward the cafeteria, leaving Janice alone in the kitchen. Janice turned and walked right toward the computer room, anxious to finish her work while Alex was occupied.

She had written down Alex's username as well as his password when they worked together, so logging in was not difficult. There was another person in the computer room when she was typing this in. She nodded to the gentleman, who looked to be in his early fifties, and opened the file titled "Updated Solar Panel Script." It was just a matter of uploading her script into this one—a simple copy/paste. Then, she would upload the newly saved "Updated Solar Panel Script" to include the modification that whenever the Ark was visible within a fifty-mile radius of Houston, the panels would reflect light toward it.

That was easy, she thought. The man to her right looked at her a few times, but there was no reason to suspect that she was doing anything illegal. *I wonder if this is even considered illegal. Are there laws up in space?* Janice briefly wondered. In her script she included that the message would change within a week. First, only a Morse code "Jeremy Genser" would appear, and then the Ark would cycle through the coordinates of a checkpoint located in River Oaks, one of the wealthiest places in Houston pre-Comet. She figured that if Jeremy was in the area—a big if—then he would see it, and maybe he could go there and it would help him. *Maybe then he'll know how sorry I am*, she thought.

Janice logged out of Alex's profile, shut down her computer, and made her way toward the exercise room.

• • •

Dustin was behind the wheel of the SUV, following David's directions to the small Thessaloniki airport. It was just after dusk when they arrived. The fence that protected the runways had long since had a nice car-sized hole cut through it. Dustin did not see any planes in motion, but did notice that the runways were cleaner than the grassy areas to their side. There was no silt or dust or muck like there was off of the runway, which told Dustin one thing: there were people here. When Dustin got closer to the large terminal, he took a right. There were old signs of Aegean Airlines and Olympic Airlines, which still stood over the large terminal building.

Dustin drove past the commercial sector of the airport—past the big floor-to-ceiling windows in the terminal where people could watch the planes come in and out. There was probably a café in there, where people used to be able to enjoy coffee. Karina peered into the windows as they passed and noticed what looked like sleeping bags on the floor, and some people watching their car go by.

"There are people living in that terminal building," Karina said flatly.

David looked over at the people. There was a little

girl with her hands on the window, but that was the closest anyone came to waving at them.

"We are going to have to move fast once we arrive at the location," David responded.

Dustin focused on driving, and sped up a little bit. He drove through rows of broken-down passenger planes and followed David's instructions to get to the hangar where the Malka family plane was hopefully waiting for them. Dustin scratched at his rough beard; it was dark and bristly and it itched since he hadn't had the time to shave it in months.

Dustin noticed evidence of people living around the airport as well, like heaps of trash and fresh tire tracks in the muddy ground. As they reached the hangar, David told Dustin to park the SUV facing out. Luckily, their hangar and the surrounding area looked deserted.

"Okay, so Ben and Esther come with me," David said. "Dustin and Karina, I want you to listen very carefully. Drive left out of here, toward the higher number airplane hangars. Then take a left, and you'll see a fueling station. I want you to empty the gas canisters and fill them up with jet fuel. There should be a sign saying 'Jet-A' or 'Jet-A1'. Get as much of it as you can and come back. Try to get 'Jet-A,' but if there isn't any left then go with the other one. Then we'll talk when you get back. There's a place to fill up the car as well, but it's in a different location. It'll take a little bit before I'm ready to put all the fuel on board, so give me a second. Honey, wait here with Benny and watch out for any cars coming toward us. Once the hangar is open and Esther and Ben are inside, I want you guys to go. We should be in the air in around fifteen minutes."

David walked over to hangar number five. Hangars four and six were closed and one of them had a lock on it. There was no plane inside. David grabbed a large set of keys and started undoing the chains of hangar five, which was locked with a comical amount of chains and locks. David had ensured that no one would get into his hangar. Unlocking and unwinding all of the chains and locks took at least five minutes.

"Dad used to be what's called a ferry flyer," Ben was explaining while the others waited in the car, looking out toward the horizon for possible enemies. "He used to buy little prop planes in his spare time, fix them up, and then fly them to remote places. I wasn't born yet, but he has a lot of pictures, and he tells me about it all the time."

"Your dad sounds pretty cool," Dustin remarked.

"Yeah, he is! The plane he has now is this old beat up Pilatus PC-12 that he bought at a police auction. Apparently it was used to fly drugs into the United States, and it even had some bullet holes in it when Daddy bought it! It's much bigger than the planes he flew as a ferry flyer, and it's way nicer. He and mom spent a little bit of time trying to fix her up and it works great. It's really cool. You guys are going to think it looks awesome."

Hopefully we'll be able to see the interior, Dustin thought, though he didn't voice this opinion.

After a few minutes the door to hangar five opened, and Karina said, "Wow. It's beautiful."

The Pilatus PC-12 was a single engine turboprop passenger plane. It reminded Dustin of the movies about the dogfights in the Pacific—the Japanese Mitsubishis against the American Grumman fighter planes. From the front, this plane looked very much like those seventy-year-old dogfighters, only larger.

"It can seat up to ten people, and it can fly around two thousand miles on one tank," Esther said.

"Wow," Dustin said.

David waved to Ben who got out and ran into the hangar. Esther reached into the glove compartment and handed Dustin a pistol.

"The safety's on," she explained. "If you shoot, try not to clench your hand. Just pull the trigger and keep your hand loose. The recoil won't change the path of the bullet—only your anticipation of it will."

" . . . Thanks," Dustin gulped, holding the heavy gun in his hands.

Esther left the SUV and Dustin handed the gun back to Karina then followed David's instructions to the fuel. It was not far. Dustin went outside and found that the few times he'd refueled the car had been good practice for this, which required use of the drill and the pump. Within five minutes he was ready to pump, and luckily the Jet-A fuel pumped smoothly and there was enough in the tank. Karina emptied out the gas canisters and they were ready to fill up, lined up neatly next to the pump. As the pump did its magic the couple kept their eyes open for possible trouble.

"If someone comes to rob us," Karina said, nervously tugging at her hair while her eyes flitted around quickly, "what should we do?"

"I say we book it toward the plane and try to get on."

When the canisters were filled they drove back to the hangar where David was performing various control and quality checks on the plane.

"Daddy's checking for holes in the plane," Ben said.

"Apparently, buddy," Dustin replied warmly, ruffling Ben's hair.

David saw Dustin and told him to bring the fuel over, and he did. David opened up the ladder hatch and brought down a few oil barrels, telling Dustin to go back and fill them up as well. There were three of them.

"Only fill them up around eighty percent of the way. We want to avoid unnecessary spilling," David called from the front of the plane.

Dustin drove back to the pump and gas reserve. They made two more such trips and when they returned from their last one they saw Esther efficiently setting up a very large sniper rifle with a tripod attached to its barrel. *Whoa,* Dustin thought. *Esther didn't tell us that she's a sniper!*

The plane's propeller had started turning and David could be seen in the cockpit furiously clicking away at buttons. Dustin could see Ben's black tuft of curly hair next to David; he was sitting in the copilot's seat. Dustin looked behind to where Esther was pointing the gun, and could see a pickup truck in the distance, moving toward them.

"It's around a mile away," Esther said distractedly.

"What if they aren't enemies?" Karina offered.

"They aren't friends," she replied.

Esther fiddled with the dials on the top of the rifle and mumbled numbers to herself about the wind, temperature, pressure, the curve of the earth, gravity, and distance to the target. Dustin and Karina, meanwhile, didn't know exactly what to do. They left their bags in the car, but the Malka family bags were there too. Suddenly, both of them jumped as the sniper rifle cracked loudly through the air.

"Dammit."

Esther reloaded and tried again, aiming for one of the tires of the truck. Dustin was amazed she was even trying to shoot—the car still looked to be around half a mile away. Ben jumped out of the plane and asked if Dustin and Karina would help him with their bags, and they said sure.

Dustin grabbed a big duffle and ran over toward the stairs of the plane. The noise of the propeller was getting louder and Dustin could feel the blades creating wind. *Maybe it's affecting Esther's shot,* Dustin thought.

The truck was getting closer. There was a second

vehicle in the distance. It was coming in on the opposite side of the airport. There was dust in the distance, kicked up from the tireless tires of men on wheels. Finally, one of Esther's shots blew up one of the truck's front tires, causing the vehicle to crash onto its side.

The sound of the propeller was devastatingly loud. David yelled from the door of the plane, but no one could hear him. He tried again, and it made Dustin and Karina turn. He was pointing at his wife and motioning for her to come, but she was concentrating on the next truck. Dustin ran over to Esther, the wind from the propellers swirling all around him.

"Esther, you have to get on the plane!" he yelled.

She couldn't hear him. He grabbed her shoulder and pointed back to her husband and she nodded and ran back, bringing the gun with her. Dustin watched as she got on the plane.

It started to move forward. David embraced his wife, kissed her, and then ran to the front where Ben was making sure the plane pointed forward. The plane was completely out of the hangar now, and Dustin and

Karina could see the truck that Esther hadn't shot. There were men in the bed, and they had guns. Their faces were completely covered.

What should we do? Dustin thought, panicked. He looked back toward the car, which would have enough gas to take them out of the situation, as long as the men didn't shoot them first.

"Dustin, Dustin!" Karina yelled, pointing back to Esther who was motioning for them to come aboard. "She's calling for us, let's go, let's go!"

Dustin and Karina sprinted toward the plane. *Huff puff, huff puff.* Dustin ran against the wind of the propeller, now invisible from moving so quickly.

Karina reached the stairs first, and with a hand from Esther, got aboard. Dustin got there second, and saw the sparks of igniting guns and heard bullets whizzing by his ears. He jumped every other step and ducked into the plane, and Esther pushed a button to close the door. As the door closed and the cabin sealed, the plane turned away from the gunmen and headed down the runway.

Esther ran forward to the cockpit, and Ben buckled his seatbelt in one of the large leather seats. Dustin and Karina did the same thing. Dustin looked over at Ben and realized it was the first time he had seen the boy truly scared.

"Benny, how are you doing, baby?" Esther's voice rang out over the intercom.

"He's fine, Esther, we need to focus . . . " The intercom went dead after that.

The plane began moving faster. Dustin could hear small duds sounding below him—bullets hitting the plane. Karina squeezed his sweaty hand tight as they were pushed back in their chairs with the force of the acceleration. Dustin looked out of the window at the gunmen shooting at the plane. There were a few more *dud* sounds on the hull as the plane rushed past the attackers, and then finally Dustin felt the plane lift off the land, climbing high to the sky and to their freedom.

• • •

It was a cool dark night. Jeremy rubbed at the stubble on his chin and looked up at the dark sky. There was no moon. *That's one nice thing about the apocalypse,* Jeremy thought. *The sky looks a hell of a lot more beautiful.* Since it had become safe once again for people to venture outside, there was virtually no light pollution from Earth. The stars were already bright this far away from any major city, but the total lack of pollution from the Texan metropolises was astounding. *On a clear night like tonight,* Jeremy thought, *the stars are as good here as they are anywhere in the world.*

Next to him, Anna had one arm over her stomach, which so far showed no sign that she was ten weeks pregnant. Her hair was in a bun, which she had just learned how to do without a hair tie—or a rubber band.

"What are we going to do, Anna?" Jeremy asked.

"I don't think we have any alternative, Jer," Anna responded, knowing he was asking about the pregnancy. "It's not like we have any doctors here."

"I guess it doesn't really matter anyway. I mean the comet might come hit Earth and destroy everything."

Anna agreed.

"I just can't believe it," Jeremy said in frustration. "Why did this have to happen now? As if our lives weren't complicated enough . . . "

They lay there together watching the stars. Then Jeremy spoke.

"Anna, you see that small light traveling across the sky?"

He pointed, trying to get her eye to follow exactly where his arm was trying to go.

"Oh yeah! It's moving so fast! What is it? It's not the comets, the ones that are coming toward us?"

"No, no. Do you remember that ship that we saw? The spaceship built by the richest people in the world?"

"It's not *that*?!" Anna replied incredulously.

"It is."

They sat for a while, watching it move. It blinked on and off for a while as it passed over the Texan sky.

"It's moving so fast," Anna whispered. "Why does it blink on and off like that?"

"Actually, I don't know. It started doing that a few days ago."

The satellite blinked on and off as it traveled quickly through the sky, taking only around five minutes to sail past their field of view. Jeremy and Anna watched it travel across the cold dark Houston sky, amidst an awe-inspiring and bright backdrop of the Milky Way and a billion billion other stars.

5

NEGLECT

September 7, 2018
Pyongsong, North Korea

Robert sat in his office discussing the nuclear and North Korean rocket weapon-integration strategies with Dr. Kang. Overall, Robert was impressed with the work North Korea had done with their launch facility. He felt confident that the integration would be complete in another week, and then they would launch the first rocket. After working with North Korea, Suri and Gerald had also helped in making their missiles a bit more efficient. Thus far, though, even if everything went according to plan, they still wouldn't have enough power to get Comet 2 completely out of the way.

"What if . . . " Dr. Kang asked Robert through Mr. Yuan, "What if we just use the remaining power to try to splinter the comet as much as possible? Then it might make the effects less devastating."

"It might, but I'm not sure we have enough energy to splinter the comet anyway. And, due to conservation of energy, the comet would still hit us with the same amount of force, which would likely do the same damage."

"Unless we made more nuclear weapons," Dr. Kang responded. "We could use more if you told us what we are doing wrong in our nuclear process. We would like to learn more about these ballistic missile capabilities."

Robert looked suspiciously over at Dr. Kang.

"Sir, I know we've talked about this already, but I don't know how to build a nuclear weapon. I'm not a nuclear chemist. I'm only here to integrate the weapons to your missiles."

"And your coworker, Major Winter? He is a part of the military. Perhaps he knows something about this process?"

Robert sighed and closed his laptop.

"Dr. Kang," Robert said, "Major Winter is a leader of soldiers. He knows nothing about nuclear weapons manufacturing. He is simply here to protect me."

"I see," Mr. Yuan replied. Robert noticed that Dr. Kang did not give Robert an answer.

I can't believe they're worrying about nuclear secrets and how to make better missiles when we don't have a viable solution to Comet 2 yet . . . Robert thought, getting back to work.

• • •

Back at U.S. headquarters under San Antonio Mountain, Suri worked frantically on her modeling software as Brighton and Chaplin walked into her office for their daily briefing with Dr. Rhodes. From Dr. Rhodes's updates, Suri had learned that the two comets were behaving more or less predictably since Vishnu could track them again. Suri sat on her side of the desk, while the two politicians, looking haggard and worn out, sat on the other end. The entire team, including President Chaplin, Secretary Brighton, Dr. Olidi, the apocalyptic scientist, Gerald Jan, and many others were also there, waiting for Dr. Rhodes to join them via the satellite communication.

The conditions on Earth were getting better with each day past the impact date, but the extreme weather conditions persisted. There were huge storms of acid rain that periodically drenched the Los Alamos hills. During the day, it was necessary to protect the skin from the sunlight due to the depletion of the Ozone layer. Suri assumed it was the nitric oxide and nitrogen dioxide that got into the atmosphere from the increase in volcanic activity around the world. Secretary Brighton found this out the hard way, when he took a walk outside. Within only one hour he looked like a lobster. Suri tried not to wince at his painful-looking skin. It reminded her of the painful burns she'd received from the explosion.

Dr. Rhodes came online and within a minute her

silvery, matter-of-fact voice sounded from the speaker phone.

"Pink hair is here," Dr. Rhodes said.

"So," Suri began, "from the explosions from the IMPs and Vishnu, we have successfully moved Comet 2 away from Earth, but not far enough that it won't hit us. We just don't have the firepower or time. Comet 3 will also hit us, and as of now we predict it to land somewhere in the South Atlantic Ocean, though understandably most of our efforts are centered on Comet 2."

Suri continued. "Currently the gas jets on Comet 2 are larger in volume than Comet 1—the one that already landed—according to Dr. Rhodes's statistics. This means that while Comet 2 is decreasing rapidly in size, it is also moving faster toward Earth, which will mean a more devastating impact . . . We just don't have the power to stop the comet." *Wow*, Suri thought, *I've never said it quite so definitively before.*

Everyone in the room remained silent, unable to

believe what Suri had said, but at the same time knowing it was true.

Cognitive dissonance, Secretary Brighton thought. The mood in the office was one of despair, and it was difficult to imagine finding a solution to save the world. With only three months until the impact of Comet 2, everyone on Earth had run out of ideas.

"I hate to say it," Dr. Olidi said, "but it might be time to start preparing to go underground."

"We are underground already!" Secretary Brighton reminded the doctor angrily. "And you know as well as I do that if Comet 2 hits then we are all doomed. There isn't a bunker deep enough to save us now . . . "

A chord of hopeless acceptance reverberated through the room, and everyone was silent. Then a surprisingly jovial voice came from the intercom of the Vishnu spacecraft. It was rare that Nia had the opportunity to be involved in these meetings at all because she was far enough away from Earth that the communication would take a full eight minutes to reach and then another eight minutes for her to respond.

But respond she did, her voice crackling through the speakers around sixteen minutes later.

"You're missing something important," Nia said in an excited tone. "I thought you guys down there would have recognized it, but then again it's so obvious that I didn't see it at first either."

Her voice disappeared again, and Suri looked around the room at the confused faces.

"The Moon! The Moon! We can use the Moon as a shield. Dr. Lahdka, please see the attached model I've sent you! If we contact Dr. Miller and get him to reorient the North Korean IMPs to move Comet 2 *toward* Earth's center, it should collide head-on with the Moon. It's our best shot—what do you think? I'm standing by waiting for your response."

Suri felt that sudden heart-sink when you realize you forgot something incredibly important. *Did I really forget to look at the Moon?* Suri thought.

"What's happening?" Chaplin asked.

"The Moon . . . " Suri said.

"The Moon?" Brighton intoned.

Suri frantically opened up her mail app to download the file Dr. Rhodes sent her and looked through the model to see what her plan was.

Dr. Rhodes's voice came in over the speaker. "Sometimes it's the biggest things glaring us in the face that we miss, but this would be amazing. Freakin' great! We might be able to save the world!"

No kidding, Suri thought. *I feel so stupid.* Since her voice was delayed, Dr. Rhodes couldn't really participate in the back-and-forth conversation. However, this didn't stop her from laughing and yelping in happiness.

"You guys realize this?!"

As Suri waited for the model to show her what Dr. Rhodes had worked out, Dr. Olidi spoke up. "Wouldn't Comet 2 colliding with the Moon be potentially devastating to oceanic tidal changes? A possible shower of comet and moon fragments raining down on Earth?"

"Honestly, we don't know the possible ramifications to our own planet if we hit the Moon with a comet twenty kilometers in diameter, but it's not likely to be too much. There might be some smaller fragments of the moon that come into the atmosphere, but it would definitely save us," Suri answered, deep in thought while looking at Dr. Rhodes's data. "The atmosphere would burn up a lot of the smaller particles. It's not a bad idea . . . "

"We can do it! What do you think, Suri? Did you look at the model? Oh, I forgot you can't respond because there's another eight minute delay, sorry! But I'm just really excited!"

Gerald Jan walked over to Suri's computer and began reading through Dr. Rhodes's model. President Chaplin looked suspicious after hearing some more of Dr. Rhodes's excitable yelps coming from the speaker.

"Mr. Jan, Dr. Lahdka," President Chaplin began, "I know that Dr. Rhodes is an excellent scientist and astronaut, but is there a possibility that she is losing her cognitive faculties up in space?"

Gerald looked over at President Chaplin and smiled. "Madam President, anyone who's been in space as long as Dr. Rhodes has is liable to go crazy. Fortunately, I don't think that's happened to Dr. Rhodes just yet. This is how she usually acts when she figures something out."

As if on cue, another spat of giddy, excited laughter emanated from the speaker, and this time Suri also started smiling. *It just might work*, she thought.

The Moon had never even entered her mind, but the more she thought about it the more it was a good idea. And it wouldn't have worked unless they were really lucky with the orbit of the Moon, which according to Dr. Rhodes it looked like they were. As the model ran through its course, under Dr. Rhodes's new bombing strategy, it looked like Comet 2 could strike the Moon.

"I need to call Dr. Miller," Suri said, "and tell him that we need to change the course of the North Korean IMPs."

"They haven't launched yet, so that shouldn't be difficult, right?" Secretary Brighton asked.

"Exactly," Suri answered, and dialed Robert's North Korean line.

The line picked up after a few rings. "Mmh?" Robert mumbled.

"Robert?"

"Hello, Suri." If he had been asleep he shook it off quickly. "How did your update with Dr. Rhodes go?"

"The Moon, Robert, we forgot about the Moon . . . The Moon!" Suri could not hold her excitement. For every second she thought about the massive satellite, she started believing that the plan could work.

"The Moon . . . what do you mean?"

"Look at what I just sent you."

Suri could hear Robert's breathing on the other line as he checked through Dr. Rhodes's work. Then Robert let loose on a course of swear words and yelling that caused Suri to stifle a small laugh. *I haven't heard Robert like this in a while*, she thought.

When Robert calmed down and lowered his voice, Suri could hear Korean voices in the background.

"How could we be so stupid?" Robert chided

himself, and he must have turned away from the phone because his voice sounded muffled. "Yeah, I know, I know. Just give me a minute with my team, and I'll get to it." Then, Robert's voice came through clear once more. "Okay, I can't believe it, but okay. So, um, Dr. Rhodes, are you listening?"

"Yeah, she's here, but she's on a time delay."

"Oh, right. Well, we are almost ready for the first launch of the Korean IMPs, so it's good we caught this now."

Sporadic Korean could be heard on the phone, along with a shuffling of papers and keystrokes.

"We have a lot of work to do, but I think it'll work, Robert," Suri said enthusiastically, already thinking about her future tasks.

"Well, I want to make sure. I don't want a repeat of the fracture event of last year. Dr. Rhodes, this is excellent work you've done. Suri, we'll be in touch."

"Goodbye, Robert."

Suri hung up the phone, and the politicians quietly

left her to begin working with her team on a new strategy to shoot the moon.

· · ·

Anna walked slowly toward the restaurant to have some food with Jeremy and Tabatha, the nurse who had spotted her pregnancy. They ate in a corner of the restaurant, and since the temperatures were beginning to come back to normal, they felt it was better to be aboveground at least during the day. The soldiers didn't always like this. The man who had taken charge after Major Winter left was a stout soldier named Hardy, and he had a knack for making everyone feel a little bit uncomfortable. Whereas Major Winter had been able to convince both Jeremy and Anna that they would be safe under his protection, this was less evident with Captain Hardy.

Hardy and his men had found some old bottles of moonshine in one of the tunnels underneath the mansion, and had taken to drinking it like water. Jeremy ate his food in silence, thinking about what to do next. He had no way to help in the effort to stop the comets, and was considering going back to Vail, Colorado. Traveling around like Dustin and Karina had sounded fun, but what if they came across more anarchists or militia? Yet staying in the mansion wouldn't work for much longer—not with Anna. Jeremy did not trust the Marines without Major Winter leading them.

"Ready for our nightly walk?" Jeremy asked Anna. Their stargazing had become a nightly habit, sort of like watching TV used to be.

"Tabatha, why don't you come with us? It's really beautiful, the stars. I don't know if they have ever been this clear."

"Okay," Tabatha started, finishing her food.

The threesome put on some clothes. Even before the comet, the nights in Texas in August would be hot enough to wear just a T-shirt, but now the temperatures at night were lower. Jeremy thought the increase in volcanic activity could have done it, since the eruptions released a lot of gases and ash into the atmosphere. These smaller particles, unlike the debris from the comet's impact, floated in the stratosphere, dimming the sunlight and lowering Earth's temperature more than previously thought. The threesome walked along until they found a cozy place away from the mansion. Tabatha walked with a slight limp, and her clothes, like Jeremy and Anna's, were tattered. She had kind eyes to go with a round face, and Jeremy figured that she was about fifty or sixty years old. He wasn't the best at telling ages.

"You're right. It is beautiful," Tabatha remarked, "even if I do feel a little bit like a third wheel here."

"Oh no, don't worry," Anna replied, rubbing Tabatha's arm.

Jeremy spread out a small blanket, and they lay down, looking up at the perpetual mass of stars spread out all around them.

"I'm from eastern Colorado, a little city called Akron, and we could see the Milky Way every night when the sky was clear. Even though it's not as bright as before the comet, it's still beautiful."

Jeremy and Anna didn't say anything, and Jeremy looked for the different constellations as his eyes adjusted to the decreased light. Finally he found Orion, the Greek hunter who fought eternally in the skies against Taurus the bull.

"What's that blinking light?" Tabatha asked, pointing to a close, fast-moving light far in the east.

"That's the Ark," Jeremy replied.

The threesome watched the Ark trail across the sky.

"That's odd," Tabatha said.

"What?" Jeremy asked.

But Tabatha just frowned, mouthing something. After a few minutes, Tabatha put her hand over her mouth.

"Oh my God," she gasped.

"What's wrong?" Jeremy asked, sitting up and looking around, thinking Tabatha might have heard an enemy.

"Look at the blinking ship. Does it look like it's blinking for different lengths of time?"

"What?" Jeremy asked.

"Now that you mention it," Anna said, "yes. It looks like it just went long, and then long, and then short, and then short . . . "

That's weird . . . Jeremy thought. *Is someone on the Ark sending a message?*

"That's what I thought, too," Tabatha said, "It's Morse code."

Whoa, Jeremy thought. "Morse code? Are you sure?"

"Pretty sure," Tabatha said.

Anna and Jeremy watched Tabatha looking up at the satellite. It looked like she was studying it.

"You can read Morse code?" Anna asked, intrigued.

"Yeah, my brother taught it to me. He was in the Navy; they had to learn it."

"What's it saying?" Jeremy asked, fully intrigued now.

Tabatha swallowed, and looked over at the couple before answering. "It's saying 'Jeremy Genser. Please Forgive Me.'"

6

COMMUNICATION

September 14, 2018
One hour north of Houston, Texas

Less than three months before impact

Jeremy speed-walked impatiently back to the mansion, with Tabatha and Anna lightly jogging behind him.

"Jeremy, will you hold on?" Anna huffed from behind.

"Come on, guys!" Jeremy said excitedly.

They went back the way they came and Jeremy rushed into the house and went to the armory—the room where they kept the guns. When he found it was locked, he ran up the stairs of the mansion and over toward one of the windows where the sentries were positioned. He found the shorter one who kept the laser pointer—the five-watt military laser pointer that shone a neon green.

"Hey," Jeremy huffed, "can I borrow your laser pointer?"

The man frowned at Jeremy.

"Why?"

"Because I want to . . . can I just borrow it?"

"Not until you give me a reason why," the man said, shifting in his seat and picking his nose.

"I want to use it to show my girlfriend a star," Jeremy lied.

The man looked down at Anna.

"Oh, her? She's alright, man. She's alright."

"Can I just use it, please?"

The man took his eyes off of Anna and stuck his hand in his pocket, producing a laser pointer that looked big enough to be a lightsaber. He handed it to Jeremy, who grabbed it and came back down the stairs, motioning for Anna and Tabatha to come outside.

"What is this about, Jer?"

But Jeremy didn't answer, not wanting the sentry or anyone else to hear. He walked outside and took them back to the clearing where they had left the blanket. Jeremy pointed the sight toward the Ark and clicked the laser on. The trio could see the bright green laser in the crisp night air, traveling for the Ark at the speed of light.

"It must be Janice," Jeremy explained. "Who else do we know who would even be on the Ark? I'm going to try to reply to her—at least let her know I saw the message."

"How can you do that with a laser pointer?" Anna replied skeptically.

"It will be pretty lucky if it actually is seen by anyone up there, but it's definitely powerful enough. It could work—and honestly it's the best shot we have. I read an article that said you can see a one-watt laser pointer from space, and this one is five watts," Jeremy responded, and Tabatha nodded.

"It makes sense," Tabatha said, "but you'll have to get pretty lucky to have someone looking down on us."

"Better chance than nothing, right?" Jeremy replied, closing one eye and aiming the laser pointer.

Anna and Tabatha watched as Jeremy aimed the laser at the blinking Ark. Meanwhile, Jeremy felt for the first time in a long time that he was more in control of his life. Living underground, even under Major Winter, was difficult because so much of his time underground was spent waiting and doing a lot of nothing. Now, however, Jeremy experienced the familiar rush of doing something important, like when he had helped Dr. Miller. The rush of adventure—even if it was falsely guided—made Jeremy's heart race and his mouth turn up in a smile.

• • •

Janice woke up in a cold sweat. She got out of her hammock and stretched, opening up the kinks in her back and neck. Sleeping on a hammock never did her back much good—and sleeping in zero gravity made it even worse. She looked at the time above the door, and it was four fifteen in the morning. There weren't technically days and nights on the Ark, but since humans were used to this, the engineers felt that this was the best plan to live comfortably until they descended back to Earth. The time and days were the same as the times of the day for Earth, and specifically Colorado, since that was the ship's launch point.

Janice looked to her father's empty bunk and frowned. He normally slept exactly eight hours a day, always wanting to please his doctors in order to live as long as possible. She still had not spoken to him much since they boarded the Ark, stubbornly keeping her silence. She tried closing her eyes and counting sheep, but it was no use. Unable to sleep, she got up to roam the halls to stretch her legs, wishing she could smell real terrestrial air, instead of the recycled air in the Ark. It tasted like plastic. She walked down a few halls, her mind wandering, until she heard muffled voices. Ahead she spotted a door with light shining from under it.

"—told us that they are planning something

completely different from what we thought before," a deep and rusty voice said.

Curious, Janice stepped closer.

"So you think that this information from Korea is correct? That they are trying to use the Moon?" This voice Janice recognized as her father's.

"It's good actually. It means they won't pay attention to the smaller diameter comet, which would leave us to do whatever we want with it. I think we should be able to steer the smaller comet into orbit. Its large density of rhodium, platinum, and rhenium means that the future civilization would never need to mine for those minerals . . . "

"Have you spoken about any of this to Kaser?" Janice's father, Charlie, asked.

"Yeah, he likes the plan."

They were silent for a time, and then Charlie spoke up again.

"What about this green light you saw?"

"I talked to Rothschild about it. He thinks it's a laser pointer. Somewhere in Texas."

"Is that really possible? It seems unlikely . . ."

"It would have to be a pretty powerful laser pointer—military grade—but if he was persistent enough in aiming at us, we could see it from here, yes."

"Is it a problem?"

"No, no problem. It won't affect any of our systems here."

"Good."

Janice gasped and heard the two inside the room stop talking. Quickly, she walked past the door to pretend she was just walking by.

"Janice?" Charlie said.

She turned around and looked at her father, before turning back and walking away. It wasn't that she necessarily had to keep up the silent treatment, but her mind was already elsewhere. *Flashing green light from Texas*, she thought. *Could it be Jeremy?*

She heard her father mutter something about her being stubborn, but she was already halfway down to the viewing dock.

The viewing dock was one of the many places where

there was no attachment to the artificial gravity wing of the ship. It was a huge glass dome on the aft of the ship, or the part facing Earth while the Ark was in orbit. As a result, the "less green but still blue" planet was always visible. Janice did not spend much time there, because it meant being in zero gravity. Zero gravity was initially a fun novelty when she first flew around and pretended to play *Ender's Game*, but she now found it nauseating and unnatural.

She went through the double doors that led to the viewing dock and felt the unfamiliar lack of gravity as all her intestines moved around a little. She grimaced. Janice watched as the floor to the viewing dock opened. She floated and looked around at the Earth. Luckily, it would only be a few minutes before Texas came into view. She watched the magnificent planet, wondering what reasoning she had used to leave it. Even though it was noticeably browner than before the comet impact hit, and it looked like there was a haze around it, it was still the most magnificent looking planet in the solar system. Janice could see huge storms, probably caused by the comet's impact or the increase in volcanic activity that changed the weather patterns. She gazed at one of them, a monstrous hurricane-looking system hovering near the Bahamas, and another off the west coast of Africa.

Janice also noticed Hawaiian Islands looking a lot larger than they once were, which must have happened because of the volcanic eruptions causing the mountains to rise higher out of the ocean.

Finally, Texas came into view, and Janice held her breath as she watched the land for a sign. Maybe she would be lucky enough to see this small piece of evidence that Jeremy was alive. It was fortunate there wasn't a storm cloud obscuring Texas from view. She waited, almost holding her breath, while Texas passed by, and right before it went out of view, Janice could see a small green dot somewhere north of Houston. She was ecstatic! In fact, she doubted if anyone in the history of the world was happier to have a laser pointer shined in her face. *It must be him,* she thought. *Jeremy's alive!*

Janice pushed herself back toward the button that would open the bottom floor of the viewing dock and got back into the artificial gravity that her body and mind wanted. Then she raced to the computer room, and started writing a new script for Alex's solar panels. She thought briefly that it might not be Jeremy—that it could really be someone playing with a laser pointer—but she had to believe it *was* Jeremy. She wouldn't truly know if Jeremy was the one receiving the messages, but she just had to trust that it was. If it wasn't, she reasoned, at least she was helping someone . . .

7

A COLLECTOR

September 20, 2018
Outside Major Winter's Mansion

"1—8—2—1—R—I . . . " Tabatha stared at the Ark with binoculars and rattled off numbers and letters to Jeremy, who wrote them down in a small notebook:

1821 River oaks boulevard stop supplies food car stop pw stop 23fne9D4HBB. I am sorry stop Janice — QSL?

Jeremy stopped writing.

"What does QSL mean?" he asked.

"It means, 'Do you copy?'" Tabatha replied, still looking through the binoculars.

Jeremy looked back at all of the information he had written and nodded to himself, then looked up at the ship. They had been copying code for three revolutions of the Arc to get the entire message. The first bit of code they received hadn't made sense, but as the rest of the message came through a few hours later, they were able to discover that this part was the ending. Then, Jeremy grabbed the scope he stole from the armory and shined it best he could in the direction of the Ark. Even though Jeremy did not have the accuracy with the laser pointer to return a message to Janice, at least she would know that someone had received her message.

"So, Janice wants us to go to this address?" Anna said, narrowing her eyes at Jeremy's notebook.

"Not that it's my business, but who is Janice?" Tabatha asked.

"We met her when we lived in Colorado, but she ended up betraying us."

Tabatha nodded, "So you think this address might have some food or tools? A way to say 'I'm sorry?'"

"It's possible," Jeremy said, frowning at his notebook.

"What do you think this address is?" Anna asked.

"I'm not sure," Jeremy answered. "In the Morse code message she said 'car' and 'food' so maybe it's a place with stocked supplies?"

"I heard a rumor that certain people built secret bunkers with survival gear and food, for after the comets hit. It could be that?" Tabatha said.

Jeremy thought about this. Could Janice be giving them the location of one of these survival bunkers? "Maybe she is trying to make up for her mistakes. Or at least, that is what someone wants us to think," Jeremy answered.

"But, how did she know we would be near Houston? How did she know you would look at the Ark, or that we would even be alive?" Anna accused. "I don't know. How do we know she's telling the truth? Or if it's even her?"

"I know you don't like her, Anna—"

"This has nothing to do with liking her, Jeremy," Anna said sternly. "I don't *trust* her."

"Well, okay then. Maybe that's why she would send this message, to regain our trust. I think she is moving the solar panels. It's sort of brilliant, actually, using the reflection of the sunlight off of the solar panels to send us Morse code. She must have figured out a way to move them to blink at us while the Ark is over Texas. It's pretty risky, because the ship will lose a little bit of solar power, and if she got caught, well . . . " Jeremy wondered what they might do to Janice for treason. Kick her off the ship? Torture her? He shuddered. "I think she feels guilty about being a spy for the billionaires. I think she's trying to make up for it, and she assumes that if we're still alive we must be around Houston since she figured that we didn't really have anywhere else to go."

"River Oaks is, or at least it was, a very exclusive neighborhood, so it would make sense if these billionaire Ark people were hiding something there for when they came back," Tabatha offered.

Jeremy looked back down at his notebook and then back up at the sky. *Can we trust you?* he wondered. He wanted to believe her—he really did. It would be nice to have a concrete place to hide out, a safe place for Anna to have their child, and they would be away from the militiamen who kept looking at Anna. But then there was the unknown.

They could encounter thugs, thieves, or murderers on their path to the address. They could get lost. The Sun could do them in, as well, or some freak tornado or other extreme weather event. Jeremy had been to River Oaks before. A friend of his from his high school basketball team lived there and used to have parties. Jeremy figured it was about an hour away—if they could drive. It would probably take a day or two to walk if they didn't have a car. He supposed it would be possible to use one of Major Winter's motorcycles, which were located in the garage of the mansion, and were used in patrol and scouting missions.

"I think we should go, and use one of the motorcycles. We could even say that we want to perform our own scouting mission and—" Jeremy spoke, until being cut off by Anna.

"You really think that Captain Hardy would let us use one of the motorcycles? Come on, Jer, I know you don't trust him. If we go, we'd have to steal the motorcycle."

At this point Jeremy and Anna both realized that they were having a "couple's argument" about what to do next, but forgot that Tabatha was still standing right next to them. She looked from Jeremy to Anna and then back, like she was watching a tennis match, and once they realized this they stopped. They both realized that Tabatha would have to come with them.

"Do you want to come with us?" Jeremy asked. He realized that there was no other way. Tabatha might tell Captain Hardy or someone else about the River Oaks address, and then he wouldn't be able to keep them safe.

Anna nodded. "Please?"

"I don't know," Tabatha began. "I don't know how to ride a motorcycle."

"We could come back for you?" Anna answered.

All three of them realized this was probably an empty promise, but it needed to be said nonetheless.

"Maybe," Tabatha replied.

They stayed looking at the ship for another revolution to make sure that there wasn't more that Janice wanted to say, but the message simply repeated itself. Jeremy flashed the laser up at the ship again in case someone was looking down on the Texan midlands, and then they walked back to the mansion.

"Thank you so much for deciphering the message for us, Tabatha," Anna said, holding Tabatha's hand in hers.

"Of course, sweetie," Tabatha replied kindly, "I won't tell where you're going, I promise."

Jeremy and Anna reached their room and filled up backpacks with food and medicine, and halfway through packing Anna looked around and suddenly started to cry.

"I don't have any clothes," Anna said.

"What? Anna you have lots of clothes."

"My pants are starting to get too tight and I can barely fit into my bras anymore. I'm peeing like fifty times a day and I'm literally *always* tired. I feel like I just got done running a marathon, Jeremy, and these hormones are making me crazy!"

Jeremy sighed, putting his arms around his girlfriend, who felt hot to the touch.

"I'm sorry, Anna. I obviously can't say I know what you're going through. But we do need to go, and now might be our last chance. If we can make it to this bunker, it'll be a safe place for us to have the baby."

Anna looked up at Jeremy.

"Are you sure? Why not stay here?"

"We could," Jeremy responded, sitting down across from Anna on the dusty bedroom floor, "but I've heard the militiamen talking, Anna, and they make me nervous. They don't have Major Winter controlling them, and I'm not sure we should trust Captain Hardy. It's risky to be outside, I know, but we won't be outside for that long."

"You really think we can trust Janice?"

"Well, I don't know why she would lie. How could us going here, with a password, give her anything? I think she feels bad for betraying us . . . "

"You're willing to risk our lives on that?" Anna countered.

"I think that staying here any longer might be risking our lives. Let's face it, we are in a no-win situation, but we have a chance. What if this is some kind of bunker for the Ark people once they get back to Earth? Janice wants to help us survive by giving us access to it while everyone else is still up in the Ark. I don't think she'd try to screw us over. And I can't think of a better place to have the baby."

"I guess you're right," Anna said nervously.

They continued packing up and they decided to leave as soon as they could. Anna found an old road map, and with everything packed up, they snuck out to the garage where Major Winter kept the motorcycles. It was padlocked.

"What now?" Anna whispered.

"Get Tabatha, and I'll be right back."

The padlock held the double doors of the garage shut with a chain—a chain which could be cut with some ordinary bolt cutters. If Jeremy was lucky, there would be some bolt cutters in the tool shed. Jeremy had gone into the tool shed to put back the shovels when he had to bury the bodies of the thieves after they died. He went into the shed and found the bolt cutters hanging on the wall by the spades. He grabbed them and walked quietly back to the garage, and cut the chain.

"Whoa," Jeremy said, when he shined a flashlight into the garage.

There were dozens of motorcycles from all different eras of production in the garage. Jeremy walked around, admiring the BMWs and the Kawasakis all lined up in neat little rows. Jeremy admired the collection of motorcycles, wondering if they were Major Winter's or the previous occupant's.

"Jeremy!" Anna whispered. "Let's just pick them and go!"

Jeremy had only the pistol for protection, with two extra rounds of ammunition. He found an old BMW R27, with the keys in the ignition. To his delight he saw there was a sidecar attached to it, which made having the two huge backpacks somewhat more bearable. Anna found an old Kawasaki which she grabbed. They filled the sidecar attached to Jeremy's BMW with their packs, and then Jeremy straddled the seat, pushing the bike forward with his toes. As planned, Tabatha came up next to them, with her own backpack, but when Anna motioned for her to get on the back of the motorcycle, Tabatha ignored her, instead thrusting the backpack in her hands. Anna gave her a look of confusion in the hazy night.

"I'm too old to be going on a life-or-death adventure, Anna, I'm sorry. I'm staying here. I just don't want to risk things here. This backpack is for you—it has as much medicine as I could find to make sure that baby stays healthy."

"Tabatha—thank you, really—but what about the militiamen?" Anna protested. "What if they want to hurt you—or worse?"

Tabatha smiled. "Honey, I think they're a lot more interested in you than in me. I'll be fine. And anyway, I know how to handle myself, don't you worry."

Anna looked unconvinced, but it was clear that Tabatha had made up her mind. Anna got off her motorcycle and hugged Tabatha, and then Jeremy did the same.

"Be careful out there, Jeremy. And take care; you're caring for three now," Tabatha said, winking at Jeremy.

"I will, I promise. Thank you for everything," Jeremy answered, clutching the piece of paper with the address and password to the bunker in his hands.

Then Tabatha left, leaving Jeremy and Anna by themselves in the garage. Once Jeremy got outside the mansion, he reached to turn the key to start the motor, but then Anna tapped him on the shoulder.

"Maybe we should just walk it until we are out of their range . . . just in case, you know?" she whispered.

"Yeah, I agree—good idea."

They walked in silence for a while, pushing their motorcycles. Then Anna climbed on and Jeremy finally fired up the engine when they figured they were far enough away. They raced into the night, heading south—back to their home city of Houston with the cold night air stinging their faces.

8

AWAY FROM HOME

September 20, 2018
Pyongsong, North Korea.

Robert stood in his North Korean jumpsuit watching cold hail pelt the runway and waiting for Gerald Jan to arrive in his private jet. Robert was cold, but it was still too early to call it winter. Gerald was coming to North Korea because it was getting to be too difficult to continue to call him in California, relay with New Mexico, and coordinate the three locations' sleeping schedules. Not to mention that Gerald could connect a little better with Dr. Rhodes than Robert could. Robert could go toe-to-toe in physics with everyone, but this Dr. Rhodes had a different way of doing things, and her status as the final decision maker on

Vishnu frustrated him at times. Robert needed Gerald to confirm the reintegration done by Robert and his team before the launch.

He had spent the last month rerouting all the rockets to force the larger comet to collide with the moon on its way to Earth. Thus far the rerouting had been a success, but often Robert found himself disagreeing with Dr. Rhodes's analysis of certain data. For example, in regards to the new Korean IMP launches, Robert, Dr. Rhodes, and Suri all had differing opinions about the precise coordinates for the paths of the missiles.

"We need to launch as soon as possible, when we are still farther away from the Sun, because otherwise we will be fighting against its gravity," Dr. Rhodes had explained in a slightly flippant tone.

"We don't know enough about the comet's vapor jets yet. We don't want to have to counter-correct," Suri had countered.

"We know enough now. We can see from our light reading that there is only a fifty-one liter per second sublimation rate, which is not causing a significant change in orbital path. If we wait too long, as Suri suggests, we may not have enough time to redirect our missile—"

"But if we shoot now," Suri interrupted, "we won't have the ability to correct at all. We might as well start praying . . . "

Robert had listened to both sides intently, and then there was a swash of Korean as Mr. Yuan translated the issue for Dr. Kang.

"I believe," Mr. Yuan had said, translating Dr. Kang's words, "that it is better to fire now than to wait. The moon plan is risky, and right now we are in the process of building more rockets. If we have to we can manufacture more nuclear weapons to affix to more Interplanetary Missiles."

Robert thought for another minute, and since he hadn't spoken yet, everyone else became quiet. He frowned at Dr. Kang's proposal of building more nuclear weapons, principally because he knew North Korea didn't have the capability to build the kinds of nukes the IMPs use, but he let that part go. It was a tense minute while everyone waited for Robert to speak.

"I agree with Dr. Kang. I agree with Dr. Rhodes. I think we need to fire as soon as possible. Our change of course strategy isn't perfect, but the nukes from Dr. Rhodes's Vishnu spacecraft have been widening the sublimation jets, and the IMPs sent from the USA will help. We are ready to fire three Korean IMPs into space now, and we'll assess their paths and determine our future courses of action."

It was incredibly challenging to make American nuclear weapons coordinate with a North Korean launch station. Of course, the United States purposefully avoided collaborating with North Korea on such matters, so there were both hardware and software difficulties to integrating the systems. For instance, Robert had to change many of the pipes by building larger attachments for them in a machine shop. It was crude, but these rockets had the benefit of being strictly one-way; he did not have to ensure these missiles came back to Earth. Their journey into space was also much shorter than their previous IMPs, since the comets were effectively in Earth's orbit, just on the other side of the Sun.

Aside from being Dr. Rhodes's home, Vishnu also functioned as a satellite to relay the information from the missiles back to headquarters in Los Alamos. Robert feared that Dr. Rhodes might take matters into her own hands, which would prove disastrous for their efforts, but he honestly did not have an option other than trusting her. He could not force her do what he wanted.

Robert snapped out of his reverie as Gerald's jet landed and taxied to where his team was waiting. A moment later, Gerald descended the stairs of his plane holding a briefcase and a duffel bag and joined Robert on the tarmac.

"Dr. Miller, how are you?" Gerald asked.

"Fine, Mr. Jan. Let's get to work. It's nice to see you."

Gerald nodded, and the two walked immediately

down to the production facility, where they oversaw the tests being conducted by the Korean engineers.

On top of everything, there were certain things that Robert had to try to keep from the North Korean scientists (Dr. Kang included) because of Major Winter.

As they looked over the data together, Mr. Yuan walked up and asked to speak with him in private.

"One of the conditions of our two nations cooperating," Mr. Yuan began, "was the help in building nuclear weapons, and improve our ballistic capabilities here for the North Korean people."

You've got to be kidding me, Robert thought.

"Listen, Mr. Yuan, I've already told you. I don't know how to make a nuclear weapon, but if I did— and if it was important to the mission of defeating the comet—you bet I would do what I could to help."

Robert actually liked Mr. Yuan but was annoyed at his persistence in telling Robert that the North Koreans wanted nuclear weapons. *Wouldn't they be happy enough with an undestroyed Earth?*

Suddenly, Major Winter walked up to him, asking

to speak with him in private. *What's with the need for private conversations today?* Robert thought.

"What am I doing here, Robert?" Major Winter asked.

Robert could smell whiskey on Major Winter's breath.

"What do you mean? You're here protecting me from harm in this country."

Major Winter raised his eyebrows. "I'm a glorified security guard, Robert. You don't need protection. These people need you just as much as you need them. They aren't going to do anything to you."

"They might when I integrate everything and they don't have a use for me anymore. They keep asking me to give up our nuclear secrets."

"And if they don't get them, they might kill you," the major replied, coolly.

"Yeah, they might, but wouldn't they torture me first?"

"It is not pleasant," the major said.

They walked along in silence and then Robert

excused himself to go to the bathroom. He walked into the urinal stall and waited, thinking about the work he still had to get done. Then he heard a voice coming from the bathroom stall next to him, and to his surprise it was in English.

"Yes, sir. I understand, sir. We are now in the process of sending the nuclear weapons, and I'll give you the data on our launch schedule. Yes, sir. No, sir. I'm sorry, sir. I know, sir . . . "

What is going on? Who is on the phone? Robert wondered, listening intently.

"The American is smart, sir, and they are launching soon. I think that they are going for the larger comet to collide with the Moon, so if you want to put one of them into orbit then—"

Just then, Robert's urinal flushed automatically, which caused the voice to stop. While Robert grimaced, wishing he could have heard the end of the conversation, he heard some quick whispering. Robert zipped up and thought, *If I leave right now he won't know who was listening to him, but otherwise I can confront him, and see who he was talking to . . .*

In a snap decision he walked quickly out of the bathroom unseen by the mysterious person, and saw Major Winter waiting for him with crossed arms.

"Quick, follow me," Robert hissed.

They hurried around a corner and peered out as a nervous-looking scientist exited the bathroom looking left and right.

"That guy," Robert whispered, "was speaking to someone in the toilet stall when I was at the urinal. He was telling someone about our plans for the comets. I don't know who he was talking to, or why, but I think I found something for you to do."

"You want me to find out what's going on with this scientist," Major Winter surmised.

"Exactly, but be discreet. I don't want him to know that we know."

"You got it, Robert."

Robert walked back to where Gerald was still

looking over the launch information, testing data against models on his computer.

• • •

One week later, Robert and the team were ready for the launch. He stood outside in the blistering cold with the North Korean oligarchs and with Suri on the phone. They were far enough from the launch site that the smoke from the liftoff wouldn't reach them. He felt haggard because the launch was at five-thirty in the morning. The Sun had just risen, and Robert watched as workers scrambled around, performing the last minute checks on things like pressure gauges, gaskets, fuel tank load, and much more.

Thus far, the IMPs had hit Comet 2 successfully, as had half of the Vishnu spacecraft's nuclear weapons. Combined with the rockets sent today and those sent in the next few weeks, it looked like a real possibility that the Earth might actually be saved! Gerald Jan was not so sure, and he advocated for bringing some nuclear physicists to North Korea to produce more weapons, which Robert was sure would be a contentious option with President Chaplin. But it was more important to save the world than keep the North Koreans ignorant of nuclear secrets.

Since the Moon was three thousand, four hundred, and seventy-four kilometers in diameter, Robert's team had discovered that the difference in mass between it and the twenty kilometer-diameter comet was too large to make any appreciable difference in the Moon's orbit. *Though it may end up affecting the patterns of our tides, which could be disastrous,* Robert thought. But it was better than a direct impact on Earth.

Dr. Kang did not like the plan, and he did not like that thus far Robert had failed to give him any real information on nuclear weapons, or on fitting them to missiles. Dr. Kang was rapidly reverse engineering Robert's work, but he wanted more. In all likelihood he was receiving threats from his superiors, and every time Dr. Kang asked Robert for pertinent information, he went off on a long tangent about the difficulties of integrating the American weaponry with North Korean missiles.

Nevertheless, Robert sat now in the command center of the launch facility with Gerald Jan as Mr. Yuan translated the intercom checks being completed.

"Bravo, go. Booster, go. Auto sequence start. Onboard computers in control of all critical functions. T-minus fifteen seconds and counting."

Five seconds later, the exhaust shoots rotated into position and sparks began to fly below the missile. Then with five seconds to go, the thrusters ignited, and Robert could hear the deafening sound of the liftoff begin.

"And liftoff!" Mr. Yuan translated, as the North Koreans around Robert began to cheer.

We're not in the clear yet, Robert thought, looking over at Gerald Jan, who looked terribly pale. *Maybe he's just stressed,* Robert reasoned.

As the rocket gained altitude, Robert watched the figures coming from the onboard computer. *Everything's looking good,* he thought excitedly.

As the missile continued to shoot into the sky and leave Earth's orbit, it fought hard against the ever-present force of gravity. This missile would have a long way to go before it would be allowed to explode. *No matter the uncertainty in life,* Robert thought, *I can always count on gravity to take me back from the clouds.*

Robert relayed what he'd seen to Suri and the rest of the team in the United States.

"Rob, this is Nick. I'm wondering how working with the North Koreans is going? Do you need any help there?" Secretary Brighton's voice spoke roughly into the phone.

"It's going well. I'm not sure how much help you would be; Major Winter already feels pretty useless," Robert said, leaving out the part where the major was working to figure out what was going on with the mysterious bathroom conversation.

Robert heard Secretary Brighton *hmph* and continued relaying technical information to Suri, sending her documents and flight analyses of the successful launch.

"One launch down, five more to go," Robert said to Gerald.

"Yeah . . . " Gerald replied, and Robert noticed his pale, sickly complexion.

"Are you alright, Gerald?"

"I think so, Robert. I'm sorry, my chest is just hurting. And my arms. I'm not sure. Also, I'm actually having a little trouble breath—"

Before Gerald could finish his sentence, he fell in a heap to the ground, clutching his chest.

"Gerald? Gerald, are you alright? Oh my God, Mr. Yuan! Call an ambulance!"

Robert got off the phone with Suri and immediately checked Gerald's pulse and heart rate. Gerald's heart was beating out of his chest and he was sweating and grimacing in pain.

"Is anyone here a doctor?" he yelled.

But it was no use. Soon, Gerald lost consciousness, and it was another five minutes before the ambulance came.

An hour later, Mr. Yuan received a phone call

saying that Gerald Jan had experienced sudden cardiac death as a result of a myocardial infarction—a heart attack. He had died on his way to the hospital.

• • •

Flying in the Pilatus PC-12 was a lot bumpier than expected. As they gained altitude, and Dustin and Karina sat in the cabin of the luxury jet, they were nervous. They weren't very high, not even close to cloud level. As they traveled over the plains of Bulgaria, Esther appeared from the cockpit. As she opened the door, an annoying beeping could be heard inside the cockpit.

"Well," she began as she walked toward the cabin, "how are you Benny? Karina? Dustin?"

Benny said, "Good, Mom," and Karina and Dustin nodded, a little shaken.

"So, we were very lucky. The shooters ended up hitting a part of the plane that, while important, obviously doesn't ground us. The only thing that doesn't work is the pressurization system of the plane. This is ironic, since it's just about the simplest system within this aircraft. Anyway, this means that we can't regulate the pressure, and it wouldn't be good for us to travel above ten thousand feet. Therefore, we have to fly low, so we'll be getting some beautiful views."

"Nice," Ben said.

"But," Esther continued, "it'll be more dangerous, because most bad weather is closer to the ground, and we can't really fly over it. We can fly around it or through it. Fortunately, for this first leg of the trip, the weather doesn't look too bad—at least for the first few hours. We may have to make one or two stops for fuel, depending on our route."

Esther then turned to Ben. "Honey, will you go join Daddy up front?"

"Why?" Ben asked.

Esther spoke Hebrew rapidly at her son, and he ducked his head and went to the front of the plane.

"You two weren't supposed to be on this plane."

"We would have died," Karina said.

"That's why I told you to come, but it's going to bring up some problems, and I just wanted to warn you. We've been in contact with the people at the Svalbard Global Seed Vault for a while, and both David and I have worked with their leader in the past. But they aren't the most trusting bunch. They think that the fate of humanity rests solely in their hands, and that if anything does not go how they expect it . . . well, they don't like it.

"Now, we will try to get as far north as we can, and hopefully make it to Svalbard. I just wanted to prepare you that these people are not going to be happy that we are bringing some new people whom they do not know personally." Esther leaned in, saying, "Even though my husband is a sourpuss, both of us trust you. I'm just not so sure about the people there. They might not be as friendly as we have been. Just to warn you."

Esther got up, thanked them, and walked back up to the cockpit, just as the turbulence started, leaving Dustin and Karina to wonder what to expect in Svalbard.

9

NEW HOMES

September 26, 2018
Just North of Houston, Texas

Jeremy was having trouble with riding the motorcycle. He knew the general procedure; the gears are under the left foot, and the clutch is on the left handle, the acceleration on the right. The problem was his practical experience, which was basically zero. Anna tried to help by yelling at Jeremy from her bike, but much of the advice was unhelpful and pitying.

"Maybe you should try . . . " Anna yelled. "You just have to *feel* it."

"I know, Anna," Jeremy said in frustration.

Why do we have to be the ones who get pregnant? Anna thought bitterly. On the other hand, the vomiting was getting less constant, which was a relief. She should be able to start seeing a change in her belly soon, at least according to Tabatha, which was exciting but also weird. Unfortunately, she still suffered from some mood swings, and a bout of constipation, which actually might turn out to be more helpful than harmful—at least on their trip.

Jeremy jerked and stalled his way down the road for a while, but then he started figuring it out and the ride went more smoothly for him. Jeremy felt a little embarrassed that his girlfriend was a better biker, and he was determined to practice. Jeremy had covered his face with a ski mask he had found in the mansion. Every part of his skin was covered, and as the Sun came up it got hot. Jeremy could feel his back sweating and the sweat dripping down his arms from his armpits. There was a tint to the land, but through his ski mask it still looked dreary and grey. There was no rain, but the weather looked stormy and treacherous ahead of them.

Those same tree spikes, the remnants of the great

increase in temperature, dotted the landscape. There were empty, dilapidated buildings as they drove into Houston. Many of the windows on the huge skyscrapers had been obliterated, and some were edged with dangerous shards, as if shattered. The buildings looked malignant, covered with a dark, sooty dirt. Jeremy thought that after the comet hit, the plant life would grow over the buildings and other marks of human civilization, but figured maybe that was still on its way.

Jeremy and Anna rode slowly to reduce the chance of slipping on the muddy road, and Jeremy tried to look straight ahead, instead of looking around at all the destruction. A few off-ramps and on-ramps brought them to the San Felipe Road exit, which led to the River Oaks community. Even though it had been three years since Jeremy had visited this part of Houston, he still remembered how to get there; it turned out they didn't need that paper map after all.

Off the freeway, the conditions of Houston could easily be seen. The city was still standing despite the devastation of what looked like a tsunami that had rushed through the city, and there was no visible vegetation—no visible green. The temperatures were still hot but not deadly during the day, but at night it was getting increasingly cooler, which was odd because Septembers in Houston were normally sweltering.

Jeremy also noticed that on a few of the houses, only their roofs were torn off. *That must have been a tornado,* Jeremy reasoned, unable to think of any other event that would take the roof off a house without also collapsing the house completely. It was difficult to tell clearly if there was any life at all in the city, but Jeremy did not see the telltale signs of fires or suspicious eyes shining back at them as they rode through the streets.

Jeremy took a left when he saw the sign for River Oaks Boulevard and remembered fondly the way the street used to look. Huge oak trees had lined the wide road, fringed by well-kept lawns and perfectly manicured bushes. The island in the middle of the road had been a neat tuft of grass, adding a spacious, dignified feel to the neighborhood.

Now the majestic oaks stood without their

branches, like columns of Hell. A fine, black layer of dust covered everything. A few blades of grass, browned to a crisp, poked out of the dust layer on the island in the middle of the road. The houses were dark and desolate, the roofs and porches covered with the same black dust that covered everything else. It was as if it had snowed soot. Jeremy and Anna counted the house numbers as they rode slowly down the street until they found 1821 River Oaks Boulevard.

"There it is!" Anna shouted over the sound of the motors.

They pulled over and gawked at the huge mansion surrounded by an ornate iron fence. There were two driveways that snaked up to the house, both of them with gates that were locked with a padlock and chains. The three-story brick house had huge arched windows and a slate roof. A covered carport housed two Mercedes sedans. There were two chimneys on either side of the house as well. Normally the house would have been partially hidden by shrubs and trees, but since the trees were now bare and the shrubs turned to dust, the house was completely visible. In fact, Jeremy could see mansion after mansion as he gazed down the street, pinnacles of wealth stripped of their excess extravagance—nowhere to hide. It gave the whole street a creepy and foreboding vibe, as if the houses were looking down skeptically at Jeremy.

Jeremy got off of the bike and stretched his legs, looking around for looters or a mob of anarchists, but no one came. Anna suggested they hide the motorcycles.

"Where though?"

"I saw a house on the last block that didn't have a fence. Maybe you could hide it behind their garage? At least someone won't assume that we are in this house. It might give us an extra minute if this doesn't prove to be helpful," Anna answered.

Jeremy nodded and rode the motorcycle to the back of the house. Then he returned and climbed one of the brick pillars in between the black ornate fence and Anna lifted the backpacks to him. He grabbed them by the straps and lugged them over the other side of the fence. Then, he stuck his hand out for Anna. She was a lot heavier than the backpacks, but Jeremy didn't mention this part to her.

"Oomph," she said, climbing up.

Jeremy jumped down to the other side and helped Anna down. They walked up to a large, beautiful red door, and tried the handle, but it was locked. There was no place for them to input a password.

"Do you think the bunker is in the house?" Anna asked.

"No idea," Jeremy answered.

Jeremy looked left and right at the property of the 1821 River Oaks Boulevard, and in the front yard it was obvious there was no apocalyptic bunker waiting for them. Just a layer of black soot. The carport to the left of the house offered no entrance, and behind the carport was a large garage which was also locked.

"Maybe it's in their backyard, or in the house somewhere?"

Jeremy nodded, and they walked back to the front of the house, where some windows were on ground level. Jeremy walked to a window, which had pre-sumably been shattered from the tsunami that rolled through the city some months before. Jeremy carefully removed a few of the shards with a gloved hand and then cautiously stepped inside the house.

Inside, he smelled something he did not expect: a damp mossy smell. In fact, when he looked at the walls in the mansion, he could see molds and even a few mosses growing. *Life!* Jeremy thought. It looked as if the house had already been vacated. There was no furniture except for a large table in the middle of the main room, where a spiral staircase coiled up to the second floor. Jeremy poked his head out and called for Anna to come inside. They left their backpacks just inside the windowsill.

Jeremy and Anna walked around the house. The smell and the lack of furniture and the mold and moss gave it the feel of being corrosively haunted.

"This place is haunted," Anna whispered, reading his mind.

Jeremy did not answer. Walking through the back

of the house, Jeremy found a smaller dining room through which two screen doors led to a private swimming pool.

"Whoever lived here was living pretty nicely," Anna commented.

Jeremy nodded. They walked past the dining room table and under two chandeliers.

When Jeremy looked in the backyard, something caught his eye, glinting from the Sun's harsh rays.

"Look!" he said, motioning toward the far end of the pool. In the corner was something that was not included in the construction of the traditional French mansion—a metallic door. The door was angled into the ground at about forty-five degrees. He and Anna hurried over to it. On the door was a ten-digit keypad.

"This must be it," he said, excited.

Under the keypad was a screen, which lit up when they came near. To Jeremy's surprise, it actually spoke to them.

"Welcome to Checkpoint 17," a sweet feminine

voice said. "Please place your hand on the screen, or input the password, followed by the pound key."

Anna handed Jeremy the piece of paper with the password on it, and he did what the automated voice told him. When he finished, the screen showed a small swirly ball which spun in place for a few seconds. Then the screen turned green and the voice said, "Thank you," and there was an audible mechanical sound as the door unlocked. Jeremy quickly jogged back the way he came, got their bags, and hustled back.

He turned the stiff handle and pulled the door open with great difficulty. "Holy crap it's heavy," Jeremy wheezed, pulling at the door with all his strength.

Stairs—that was all Jeremy could see. He stepped down into the bunker first, gun in hand, and walked down the metallic steps, Anna in tow. Fluorescent lights on each side of the stairs lit their way, and when Jeremy reached the last stair, he heard the door close behind them.

"Please reset the password at the computer to your right," the same soft voice called from a speaker.

Jeremy looked around. He was in a small room lit by fluorescent lights. It was square and low-ceilinged and it was nearly precisely what he had expected, only better. Lined along the northern wall, to Jeremy's left, was a row of weapons: pistols, assault rifles, and even two swords. On the southern wall was a door, and to the sides of the door were several more pieces of defensive equipment, but also farming equipment—hoes, tilling equipment, shovels—and built into the wall were multiple little drawers. There was a faucet for filling water bottles, too.

Through the southern door was a pantry, filled with all types of preserved foods.

"God," Anna said upon seeing the store, "they were really prepared. All this food could last for years. And it looks untouched. It makes sense that this would be a place for the billionaires to go after they return to Earth."

Next to the pantry door there was another door, inside of which was an array of cots and a bookcase full of engineering books. Located next to this bookcase was a big chest, which Jeremy opened. He looked down at rings, photos, old postcards, family heirlooms, and keepsakes of the people who intended to return. There was a small stuffed bunny, a photo book showing an older man and a woman playing with two young children, and several flash drives. After perusing the photo book, Jeremy felt like he was intruding too much on whoever had put the personal items there, and put it aside.

Jeremy walked back to the main area of the bunker and stood at the computer, filling in a new password. *If anyone else reads the message,* Jeremy thought with relief, *at least now they can't get in.*

Jeremy fiddled with the computer for a bit, seeing what he could do. It was very advanced, and had digitized copies of the engineering books that were on the shelves. There were "how-to" manuals on everything from agriculture to semiconductor manufacturing processes. There were also two surveillance cameras outside which allowed Jeremy a view of the bunker and the front of the house. On the east side of the wall was a door much larger than the pantry or the bedroom doors. Jeremy walked over and opened it to find a large garage with a military-grade Humvee parked inside. The garage was also a full-service machine shop, with tools of all kinds hung neatly on the walls. It reminded Jeremy of when his father would tell him about his dream workshops. He began to imagine his father there with him, admiring the vast array of tools.

"Jeremy, check this out!" Anna called from inside the pantry.

Jeremy came back from the shop and his daydream and saw Anna. She was pointing to a set of drawers labeled, *Seeds*.

"Seeds?"

"Not just seeds, look," Anna said, and recited, "UV-B tolerant Golden Cross Bantam—Corn. UV-B Tolerant Early White—Onion.' These must be genetically modified crops that can withstand the harmful effects of the Sun."

Jeremy was blown away. "That's amazing! It seems like these billionaires knew what they were doing."

"Almost," Anna giggled. "They didn't expect us to find it."

. . .

The plane ride was one of the most beautiful, bumpy, and frightening flights of Dustin's life. Since the plane could not be pressurized, they had to fly over the countryside. They flew low, and as a result, the view out the window was one of the most beautiful things Dustin had ever seen. They still flew fast—around three hundred miles per hour—so watching the ground below whisk by as if they were a flying bird was breathtaking.

The flight was also very turbulent: since they had to fly close to the ground, it also meant they had to fly in heavy winds. Suffice it to say if there had been nervous flyers, they would have needed the vomit bag on multiple occasions. Of course, Ben slept almost the entire flight, or remarked on how the turbulence reminded him of a roller coaster.

They were now somewhere over Sweden, having

gone around the Alps, and would need to refuel somewhere in Norway before they traversed the Arctic Ocean. Ben was asleep and Dustin and Karina were alone together in the cabin. They were playing Go Fish with a card deck Karina had found in the cubby in between their seats.

"Got any fours?" Dustin asked.

"Go fish, baby."

They sat quietly playing. They would land in just under two hours. Dustin would again help David refuel and get back in the air as quickly as possible.

The time passed slowly but eventually they started their descent and Dustin watched in amazement as the islands and archipelagoes of southeastern Norway raced by them.

"There are so many islands," Dustin remarked.

"Norway has over fifty thousand islands!" Ben commented.

Their descent, Dustin noted regrettably, was over water. It reminded him of flying into San Francisco International Airport where he'd once had a similar nerve-wracking feeling. *There's no land*, he thought. *We're supposed to land on . . . land!* Dustin leaned forward. The wing obscured much of his view, though he could see a bit of a city.

Their landing was a bit bumpy. To Dustin's great surprise, when they reached the end of the runway and the plane had slowed down, he saw an air traffic controller using the huge light-up batons—the kind he used to call lightsabers when he was younger—to direct the plane.

"Look, Karina!" Dustin said eagerly.

Karina opened her mouth in surprise. *Could this be just a normal, pre-anarchy city?* Dustin wondered. As they slowed down and began to taxi down the runway, they could see other air traffic controllers waving the plane this way and that.

Dustin got up and walked to the cockpit, and knocked on the door.

"Come in," David uttered.

"Hi, I just had a question," Dustin began as David focused on steering the plane in the direction the aircraft marshals told him to go. "Is this somehow a normal city? Has it been not ruined by the comet or anarchy or anything?"

"This city is called Bodo, but I'm not exactly sure. Many islands farther out from the Scandinavian mainland sheltered Bodo from the tsunami, and knowing the Norwegians I'm sure they had a bunker and shelter system in place for when the temperatures got too hot . . . The main question now is how they will treat us."

Dustin looked out of the window and saw the workers a little more clearly—they wore clothes to shield them from the Sun, so it was difficult to see their faces. The plane slowly rolled to a stop, and when it was completely still, Esther opened the cockpit door and entered the cabin. David joined her and opened the hatch for the staircase to pull down.

David looked over to Dustin and Karina. "I'm guessing you don't have passports."

"We do," Karina answered. "American ones."

Esther and David looked at each other.

"Just in case, it might be better if you two hide in the bathroom," David coaxed.

Dustin frowned, wondering why they would need to hide, but did as David suggested and crammed himself into the tiny bathroom with Karina.

"You want to . . . " Dustin said suggestively. "I've always wanted to join the Mile High Club."

Karina rolled her eyes at Dustin. "Yeah, well, we aren't a mile high, are we?"

The stairs released hydraulically and then Dustin heard footsteps coming up the stairs.

"Good evening, gentlemen and ladies, and welcome to Norway," a voice said. "Please show me your documents and please tell me the reason for your visit."

Dustin then heard David's voice. "We are going to Svalbard. My wife, Mrs. Malka, is a phytopathologist. We were also hoping to get fuel, here, sir. Do you sell it?"

"We have fuel, but I'm sorry sir, it is not for sale," a third voice said. *There must be two guards,* Dustin thought.

David walked over to the back of the plane, and out of a crack in the bathroom door Dustin could see him returning to the front of the plane with something large in his hands.

"Would you be interested in a trade? In exchange for a full tank—and our reserve tank as well—I can offer you this."

"What is this?" one of them asked.

"Must not have worked that well if they don't even know what it is," Dustin whispered.

"Shh!" Karina returned.

"*Landscape with Obelisk*, by Govert Flinck," David said impressively.

"And?" the shorter guard asked after a brief pause.

"We should speak to Mr. Christiansen," the taller one asserted. "It's called *Landscape with Obelisk*?"

"Yes, take it and show it to this Mr. Christiansen," David replied. "I'm sure he will agree to my terms."

Dustin could hear the guards walking back down the stairs and out of the plane.

"What's *Landscape with Obelisk*?" Dustin asked Karina as they got out of their hiding spot.

"It's a very famous landscape by a Dutch painter named Flinck. It was stolen in 1990 in Boston. I think the reward for information leading to its capture is, like, five million dollars. At least, before the comet it was," Karina answered, looking over to David for affirmation.

He nodded.

"Wow, how did you know that?" Dustin asked, raising his eyebrows. *Who exactly were the Malkas?*

"I watched a documentary about stolen art in sophomore history."

David explained why he was sure that the painting would get them their fuel.

"I flew a single engine Cessna out of this airport five years ago and met one of the owners of this airport, a man named Jacob Christiansen. We spoke for a few minutes about famous art, specifically paintings. I think that he will help us. At least, he should."

A few minutes went by as the group sat idly, and

Dustin and Karina sat close to the bathroom in case they had to hide again. Then there were some noises underneath the plane and David's face broke into a smile.

"They're filling her up!" he said, excited.

An old man walked up the stairs to the plane, and Dustin and Karina returned to their hiding spot.

"Mr. Malka, you do come with surprises," said the old man. "I had not expected this. How did you get this?"

"An old friend," was all David said.

The two reminisced while the plane was refueled, and then the man went back down onto the runway, allowing Dustin and Karina to come out of their hiding spot. Before long they were back in the air, making the most dangerous part of the journey: seven hundred and forty-three miles gliding over the perilous Arctic Ocean at only ten thousand feet.

10

AN UNUSUAL WELCOME

October 2, 2018
Arctic Ocean

Fortunately for everyone aboard the Pilatus PC-12, the inclement weather so common everywhere else was not present on their way to Svalbard, and they enjoyed a quick and comfortable trip. After a few naps, bathroom breaks, and staring at the stormy sea below them, the Pilatus PC-12 made its final approach to the island of Spitsbergen, the largest island in the Archipelago of Svalbard. Dustin had the idea that once they landed he should kiss the ground—like in the movies. Dustin looked out of the window at an enormous valley, rugged and brown, and as they began their descent Dustin noticed the sea levels must have risen substantially, because the water had almost risen to the point of the landing strip. Luckily, the runway was dry and safe for landing.

Once they landed, David and Esther stepped out of the cockpit and walked over to Dustin and Karina. David spoke first.

"So I spoke with Esther, and I think it would be good for you to show these people your passports, identifying you as American citizens. You can't be researchers alongside Esther because they would ask you to prove your knowledge on the subject of either seeds or plant pathogens. You can't really pretend to be our children because, well, you both look nothing like us. That gives us two options: one, we can claim that you are our lab techs, which means that you'll be put to work here, and we'll repay you with food and safety.

"The second option," David continued, "is you hide here until you are found. You were stowaways and we had no idea who you were, where you came from, or what you were doing in the first place."

"And what happens in that scenario?" Karina asked.

"I have no idea," David answered truthfully.

Dustin looked over at Karina and tried to figure out what the best course of action should be.

"Can we talk alone for a minute?" Karina asked.

"Of course," Esther responded.

Karina and Dustin walked to the back of the plane as the Malkas gathered their things and prepared to deplane.

"What do you think?" Karina asked.

"I honestly have no idea, but I am tired of hiding. I think we should face the music and accept whatever's coming. It's not like they're going to kill us or anything." *I hope.*

"Okay, then."

Karina and Dustin walked back to the Malkas.

"Put us to work," Dustin said. Karina squeezed his hand.

David and Esther nodded forebodingly at each other and then the door opened. Instead of kind-looking Norwegian officers, there were two large guns pointed up at them, and a cold breeze chilled their bones.

"State your business on Svalbard," a cold female voice hissed at them from below the descending stairs.

"Esther Malka, phytopathologist. Is that you, Lukas?"

"Esther, my God," the man said, lowering his weapon. "I did not expect to ever see you again. You picked right by marrying a pilot. Is that you, David?"

"Hello, Lukas."

"And who is this, and who are they? I'll need to see all your party's passports, if you please."

"Of course. This is Benny Malka, our son. And this is Dustin and Karina, our lab techs."

Dustin and Karina pushed themselves into view, and the guns turned to them as well. The man called Lukas stood inspecting the passports with one hand, and holding an assault rifle in the other. Slowly Dustin gave him the two passports. The man began inspecting them.

"Well, I think you know what we have to do," Lukas said cheerily.

No one responded.

Lukas took one more look at the five of them and then ushered in a few other guards to take the supplies in the plane.

"Very well," Lukas said. "Esther, please make yourself comfortable. Edgar will take you to your rooms, and there you can rest for a few hours. I will come by then, and you can begin by telling me what pathogens are inside my *Aristolochia grandiflora* seeds."

The Malkas thanked Lukas for his hospitality, and then Lukas looked over toward Dustin and Karina.

"Now, if you two would please follow me, we have some things to discuss," Lukas said calmly.

Dustin and Karina looked back to Esther and she nodded encouragingly, so they both followed Lukas out of the airplane.

"What about our bags?" Karina asked.

"Adar will take care of that for you," Lukas responded.

Dustin, followed by Karina, stepped out onto the stairs; it was freezing. They had dressed with all their layers, making their backpacks considerably lighter, but the wind still bit them to the bone. Outside, the Arctic Ocean danced in front of them, and mountains surrounded their entire horizon. The sky was dark gray, and in front of them the Svalbard Airport terminal was painted an ominous black.

As Dustin followed Lukas, he saw one of those directional signposts, which showed how far big cities were from the sign. Dustin read one of them: Tokyo—6830 km. On top of the Tokyo sign he read their current location: Svalbard Lufthavn—78°15' N 15°30' E. *Jesus,* Dustin thought, *we're only ten degrees below the North Pole. No wonder it's so cold.*

"This place looks like Hoth," Dustin said.

"What?" Karina asked, confused.

"*Star Wars?* You know, the planet with the AT-ATs?"

"I have no idea what you're talking about . . . "

He decided to let it go and continued following

Lukas to an old Saab four-wheel-drive truck. The man drove them directly toward the valley in the snow and did not say a word to them.

"Where are we going?" Dustin asked, but was met with only silence.

They traveled up in elevation, and Dustin looked around at the surroundings. Dustin imagined that before the comet he would have been surrounded by tall snow banks and snow-covered slopes. Instead, everything was mud and rock. Dustin stuck his hand out of the window and felt the wind rushing through his fingers until the wind was too cold and he rolled the window back up.

Lukas drove quickly through the valley. In five minutes Dustin could see the entrance to what must be the Svalbard Global Seed Vault—a big metallic rectangular tumor jutting out of the side of a mountain, with a short walkway built to a small unadorned door. It looked like Superman's Fortress of Solitude, if Superman was evil. Dustin could see a fenced walkway leading up to it. *Whoever runs that place has to have a fluffy, evil-looking cat in his lap*, Dustin thought.

"Is that it?" Dustin asked.

Again there was no response.

Instead of heading left toward the entrance to the Global Seed Vault, Lukas kept driving along the valley. He took a left about a minute down the road, and they came to a small parking lot with space for only three cars. One was already taken by a small Fiat, and the other was a handicapped space. Lukas parked in the third spot.

Above the parking lot was a door, which opened without a lock.

"Right through here, please," Lukas said, ushering them into a dark hallway.

Dustin could feel his heart rate increasing and felt much more nervous without the surefire Esther holding a gun at their side, and Karina felt the same way. She grabbed hold of Dustin's hand.

"Left, into this room, please," Dustin heard Lukas say from behind him, and he did as he was told.

It's going to be okay, Dustin repeated to himself. *It's going to be okay.*

He went in and noticed a small incandescent light bulb hanging from the middle of the ceiling, over a small metal table. There were two metal chairs on one side of the table and one on the opposite side. Dustin figured it would be appropriate to sit down at the two-chair side with Karina and did so while Lukas sat at the other.

Lukas removed a package of cigarettes from the breast pocket of his shirt and took off his gloves to grab one out of the package. It was much hotter in the room than out in the hallway, and Dustin took off his jacket.

"We're not here to steal anything," Karina blurted anxiously.

"That's good," Lukas replied in the same calm voice.

Lukas lit the cigarette and offered it to Dustin and Karina, who shook their heads.

"No, thanks," Dustin answered.

There was a knock at the door. A large, rugged, Scandinavian woman in a fur coat entered.

"Karina, would you please follow Astrid?"

"No," Dustin said, leaping to his feet defiantly. "You are not splitting us up."

At this, the ever-calm Lukas pulled out a pistol from his puffer jacket.

"Don't worry, Dustin, you'll see Karina again very soon. We just need to ask you both a few questions. She'll be by your side soon enough," Lukas breathed.

Karina let herself be led out by a smiling Astrid, and the door sounded right next to Dustin's ear when it closed. Lukas put the gun down on the table and took a large drag off of his cigarette, making the ember at the tip glow a fiery orange. Surprisingly, Dustin and Lukas were not the only people in the room. Since it was so dark, Dustin had not noticed another man with no emotion in his face standing all too still in the corner. The man walked behind Dustin.

"What are you—" Dustin began, but before he could finish the man had grabbed Dustin's wrists firmly and tied them behind his back with a rope. He could not get off the chair.

"Shh, shh, shh," Lukas said. "I'm only going to ask you a few questions. Thank you, Jonas."

He took another long drag of his cigarette and stood up, exhaling the smoke above him. Dustin could see the incandescent light bulb play with the smoke, making shadows dance on the floor and the table. Dustin felt his legs being tied by the man called Jonas. Dustin watched as Lukas slowly walked over to Dustin's side of the table.

Then, Lukas reached up and grabbed Dustin by the neck. Dustin struggled and fought, all while watching Lukas's hand with the cigarette which was approaching his face. Dustin screamed and his eyes opened wide as the burning cigarette dug into the flesh of his neck.

Dustin jerked his head trying to get away from the burning but Lukas and Jonas held him. It kept burning and burning as Dustin kept screaming, as if the burning might sear through to his throat, his artery, his spine. Then Lukas let go, and the cigarette hung on

Dustin's neck, still singeing him. After another second it fell down onto his pants, still lit.

Dustin breathed heavily, the pain still fire, but he regained control. He realized that he had drooled over himself while the cigarette burned him. He couldn't even clean himself up. Lukas returned to the other side of the table and lit another cigarette.

"I swear to God I'm working for David and Esther," Dustin breathed, speaking slowly.

"I know."

"What do you want from me? Why are you doing this?" Dustin said, trying to keep his heart rate low.

Lukas gave the newly lit cigarette over to Jonas, and Dustin felt the searing pain of the cigarette being put out next to the other bloodied hole in his skin and he screamed again.

"Please, please. I'm working for David and Esther," Dustin cried. "We met them in Israel. Whatever you think we are, we aren't that, I promise. We just want to live . . . we just want to live."

Lukas lit another cigarette, and then grabbed a small pocketknife from his jacket pocket.

"People always think that sharp knives are the best, but sometimes it's the dull ones that do the most damage."

"What do you want from me? What do you want from me? Ask me something, please. I'll tell you whatever you need to know . . . " Dustin sobbed, scared, thinking of how comfortable the Pilatus PC-12 had been. Karina was sitting on one of the plush seats in his mind. *Karina!* Dustin's heart jumped a beat, hoping—praying—that Karina wasn't going through the same ordeal as him.

"Why are you here?" Lukas asked, ever calmly, playing with the pocketknife.

"We want to live. I promise we are going to do whatever you say. I'm from Houston . . . " Dustin told the man everything he could tell, everything that was on his mind.

The man walked solemnly over behind Dustin. Dustin could feel the blade of the small pocketknife against his cheek, digging deeper. Dustin was pleading and pleading.

"We aren't here to steal anything! Please, what do you want from me? What do you want from me? I swear—I swear we will do whatever you want . . . whatever you want! Please! Stop!"

But Lukas wouldn't stop.

There was a knock at the door a second later, and Lukas said cheerfully, "Come in!"

Astrid returned, wiping her hands.

"Excuse me a moment, Dustin," Lukas said, ruffling Dustin's hair.

Dustin sat in the chair, conscious of Jonas standing a few paces behind him. He heard the others speaking just outside the door. Dustin looked at the incandescent light bulb. *I wonder how many years that light bulb has been on?* he wondered.

Then Dustin heard the door open again and Lukas came inside. He walked over slowly toward Dustin and put his hand on his chin, lifting his face up. The man looked kind.

"All right, then. Follow me and you can see Karina."

Jonas stepped behind Dustin and untied his wrists, which were raw from struggling against the rope. His ankles were the same way. Then Dustin walked delicately outside the room and saw Karina. He ran up and hugged her.

"Oh, Dustin," she cried.

"You're okay, Karina," was all Dustin could say.

Karina was not bleeding or burned, and she cried harder when she saw his wounds. After their brief reunion, they followed Lukas down a long dark hallway, and to a small room.

"What did they do to you?" Dustin asked.

But Karina wouldn't answer. Instead they walked along.

Inside the room they found a large bed and a table with their bags on it. They had been rifled through and their clothes lay on the bed. Undoubtedly someone had checked their things to make sure they didn't contain anything illegal. They moved their clothes off the bed and fell asleep holding each other tightly.

The next morning, Dustin woke up to a knock on the door. He got up groggily and walked over to a small pull-switch, which turned on an incandescent light bulb hanging above the middle of the room. Then he walked over to the front door and opened it.

Esther stood looking at him, a mix of pity and understanding across her face. She wrapped her arms around him.

"Good morning, Dustin. I'm sorry."

"You knew that would happen?" Dustin asked, trembling a little from the memory of the night before.

"There was no way they would trust you just from our words. They needed to make sure you were telling the truth. I didn't know of any other way. I didn't tell you because, well, I think it's best not to know exactly what's happening in the future if torture is on the agenda."

Dustin cringed when he heard the word.

"Listen," Esther said, gently holding both his

shoulders, "it's going to be okay, trust me. It could have been a lot worse. There's a bathroom down the hall. Why don't you go there and clean up, then tell Karina to do the same. We are having breakfast in one hour. Again, I'm so sorry, the people here just don't trust outsiders, and they needed to make sure you weren't lying."

Dustin nodded, attempting a smile, and then he watched Esther sigh before walking down the hall away from the bathroom. He got his towel, some soap, and a fresh change of clothes, then headed to the shower, more than happy to wash the blood off his neck and face.

11

MISSILE DEFENSE

October 10, 2018
Pyongyang, North Korea

Robert paced around in his room, stealing glances at his computer screen as he did so. He held his drink of cold amber scotch to his head, using the drink as an ice pack. Robert called the only number that he could dial, the Los Alamos National Laboratory, and asked for Suri. Since it was relatively safe to be outside again, the U.S. team had moved from San Antonio Mountain back to Los Alamos. Robert had already been in communication with both Gerald's California team and the NASA team at Los Alamos about the deaths of one of the most influential leaders in the fight against the comet.

He had ensured them that Gerald's death was not at the hands of North Korea—that he'd watched Gerald have a heart attack himself. Gerald was around fifty years old, and he'd worked more or less every hour of his waking life. Robert thought it was probably all the stress that killed him. Sometimes, he wondered why it hadn't gotten to him as well.

"Hey, Suri."

"Uh oh, what's wrong?"

Tomorrow was the day that the first Korean missile in the row of six nuclear missiles would hit the comet, which would steer its trajectory toward the Moon. Robert had been working tirelessly on this plan. Robert's head hurt, and he found himself sitting in his hotel room suite, looking out at the rainy Pyongyang skyline.

"No, no. Everything is on schedule."

"Oh, okay then. What's up?" Suri asked while trying to find her glasses. She was tucked into the covers of her Los Alamos bed, having tried to steal a few crucial hours of sleep before returning to work.

"I just wanted to hear a familiar voice," Robert said wistfully.

Robert hadn't shaved in a long time and accumulated a large white beard to accompany his unkempt hair. He looked like a fugitive in hiding, or a homeless man. He rolled the scotch glass back and forth on his temple, feeling the condensation from the ice wetting his brow.

"I miss the old times, Suri. I miss waking up and going to work, and driving home and watching *Seinfeld.* I miss going to the University of Texas to give a guest lecture to a bunch of stoned undergraduates. I even miss traffic, Suri. *Traffic.*"

Suri, surprised by this side of Robert, didn't know what to say, but was reminded of her own thoughts about life before the comet.

"I miss sitting at my computer and just looking for extrasolar planets," she found herself saying. "I miss food, real food, and not these ready-to-eat military meals. I miss . . . my parents."

"I miss my daughter," Robert said, staring at the rain.

They sat on the phone together, Robert looking out at Pyongyang, and Suri in her small room in Los Alamos. Suri started to cry softly.

"You know that whatever happens," Suri said, "you did your best."

"Yeah," Robert replied, finishing his drink. "Yeah. Thanks, Suri. I'll call you tomorrow with a status update."

. . .

Suri woke up feeling surprisingly refreshed, even though her eyes were a little puffy from the previous night's conversation with Robert. She got up and got dressed, careful to wear clothes shielding her sensitive skin from the sunlight. She lived outside now, favoring the gloomy outside to the underground. "Anywhere but underground," was what Suri said when Brighton asked her if she wanted to live in one of the small huts erected outside the National Laboratory.

She got to her office to find Dr. Rhodes's update on the explosions from the Korean missiles already in her mailbox.

Hi, Suri! I hope you're doing well. Pretty soon I'll be close enough in contact with Earth that we'll be able to have simple conversations! You have no idea how much that excites me to have a normal conversation with someone . . . but anyway: I have my telescope trained at the nuclear missiles and it looks like they'll hit the comet in around two hours. Everything is on course for success.

Suri responded quickly:

Excellent news! I'll send the information along to Robert. I'm sure he'll be overjoyed. And we'll have that normal conversation soon, Nia, I promise.

Suri picked up the phone and called Robert to tell him, and he echoed her excitement. Neither of them spoke about the conversation they had had the night before.

"So at the current rate, we are projecting that the next three blasts should put Comet 2 in the path of the Moon. Then, since Dr. Rhodes still has four nuclear bombs left on Vishnu, we can use those in case Comet 2's path is altered by the gaseous jets or anything else."

Robert thanked Suri for the update and then hung up the phone in his Pyongyang hotel room. Robert rubbed his temple and took off his glasses. He breathed on them and then wiped them with the bottom of his shirt. He looked pleased. Everything was going according to plan. He was still in North Korea, working for a government that had dealt with the comet hitting the Earth about a thousand times better than the United States, supposedly the most powerful country in the world. He had experienced a rather terrifying year—like the rest of the world—but everything was going according to plan, which excited him.

Of course, Dr. Kang and Mr. Yuan were getting more persistent by the day for nuclear and ballistic secrets which neither he nor Major Winter had. There was the chance that they would get aggressive. He wondered if they would try to keep him in North Korea, or hold him hostage until the U.S. gave up their secrets. *A day at a time*, Robert thought, calming himself.

12

BEN'S QUESTION

October 20, 2018
Houston, Texas

Six Weeks to Lunar Impact

Jeremy leafed through the journal to a blank page and began to write:

Day 24 inside 1821 River Oaks Boulevard bunker.

Life is slow here. I have begun writing a journal again—I think the last update was around a year ago or so . . . Anyway, life's been a little hectic since then. For the past three weeks, though, we haven't been up to much. I'm back in my home city! But it feels entirely different from the one I grew up in, with good reason: I've moved up in the world. I am now living in the prestigious River

Oaks community, the wealthiest area in all of Houston. It's true what they say, that once you are at the top, you find your friends are nowhere to be found . . .

Joking aside, there's no one here in Houston—not that I've seen anyway. Anna and I are living in a bunker built by billionaires, and it has all the necessities of survival, but it's lonely here. Anna is around three and a half months pregnant. We are pretty sure she got pregnant sometime in early July or late June, which would mean she will give birth in late March or early April. We might all be turned into space dust before then . . . we'll have to see.

It makes me nervous that we won't have a doctor for her birth. I am scared for our baby and for her, and for me. Since we have the huge Humvee, maybe we could go to Los Alamos, New Mexico, where Robert said the government is located. I bet they'd have doctors there. This way, maybe we could be involved in creating a New World Order . . . but now that I'm thinking of it, we definitely shouldn't name it "New World Order." That sounds pretty evil.

I'm surprised that Janice helped us find this place, and

I hope she isn't being punished up there in the sky. The Morse code has stopped coming. I've not exactly forgiven what she did by betraying us and giving up information to the billionaires, but I think helping us was a good thing.

What are we supposed to do here? We can't just live until the resources are used up and wait to die. We should find other people and help them. We should become a part of a new community.

Then again, the resources here are pretty nice. We have access to all types of heat-resistant and UV-resistant seeds, food, farming methods, soil test equipment, engineering books, a full machine shop (my father would be proud), rope, clothing, books, solar panels, and a lot more. A few days ago I used the compaction and density tester, as well as the soil analyzer, and unfortunately it looks like the River Oaks community is not ideal for farming . . .

"Jer! Jeremy!" Anna's voice called from above the open hatch in the bunker.

Jeremy's heart jumped into his chest and he closed his journal, neglecting to fold the corner to remember where he was, and rushed out of the room toward the main room.

He took the stairs by twos until he reached the hot Houston air, made even hotter by the new post-comet sunlight, which felt like it was even hotter during the day than before.

With his hand on the pistol tucked into his waistband, Jeremy looked around wildly for a villain—but saw only a giddy Anna holding her belly.

"Anna, Jesus," Jeremy said, taking his hand from his pistol, "you scared me."

"Come quick!"

"What?!" Jeremy said, worriedly rushing over.

Anna grabbed Jeremy's hand and put it over her belly.

"I think I just felt her kick!"

"How do you know the baby's a she?"

"I don't, but I'm guessing," Anna joked.

"Oh my God," Jeremy answered, his eyes full of wonder, forgetting he was annoyed at Anna for scaring him. "That's . . . really amazing, Anna."

A little jolt of excitement zipped through Jeremy. The baby, his baby, was moving inside Anna. *Hello, baby*, he wanted to say.

"Happy Birthday, Jer," Anna said warmly. "I love you."

"I love you, too," Jeremy replied, hugging Anna. He had neglected to remember that it was actually his birthday, but could not think of a better birthday present in the world than knowing his child was alive and well.

· · ·

Dr. Nia Rhodes's journal, forty-one days to Lunar Impact:

Hello again. I am continuing to revolve around Comet 2, our harbinger of destruction! I have finished all of How I Met Your Mother, *and I am very mad at the ending! It was just too sad.*

I am now looking for a new book to begin reading. I think I'll try the novel The Metamorphosis, *by Franz*

Kafka. All of the English majors I know talk about Kafka like he is some kind of god. I guess we will see for sure. I hope his books aren't too depressing. Anyway, our first explosions have ignited successfully! It looks like the Earth might really get saved, but it's going to look a lot different. As far as my work, I have five nuclear missiles left, so I will continue to orbit around Comet 2, ensuring it hits right smack in the middle of the Moon to save that beautiful blue planet of ours.

Since this is just a journal, and since I've had a little extra time on my hands, I did some calculations and modeling about what will happen after Comet 2 impacts the Moon, and I came to an interesting conclusion:

So, the impact will create a large amount of debris— part comet and part moon—that will be ejected from the surface of the Moon. And, since the Moon doesn't have an atmosphere like Earth, or as strong of a gravitational field, that ejecta will probably end up being sent toward Earth.

Now, on the way to Earth, there's that large ship that I've been told about—the Billionaire's Ark. I asked Suri to send me the orbital path of this "Ark," and it turns out it's pretty likely that this ejecta will hit it. And this ejecta, though most of it will burn up in the atmosphere and won't have too much of an effect on Earth, would absolutely destroy the Ark. Wouldn't it be ironic? The billionaires left Earth because they thought space would be safer, when in fact it's in space they are all killed by the very comet they were trying to avoid? I guess it would serve them right . . .

If we stop this larger comet, there's a new world coming. I hope that the same people that ruled the past era don't rule the next one. I'm not saying I want all those people to die—that would make me seem a little heartless—but I can't deny the fact that maybe Earth would be better off without them. Even though the comet nearly destroyed the Earth, it was pretty close to destruction anyway. Maybe this is all good. Maybe we're giving the Earth another chance, a fresh start.

Oh, I hear one of my alarms beeping. That means that I have to go fix something, so, my dear reader, whoever you are, until next time . . .

. . .

"Robert, I need to speak with you," Major Winter's voice called from the hallway in Pyongsong.

"Come in," Robert called.

Major Winter sat down with a notebook in front of him, a curiosity which Robert refrained from inquiring about.

"I found out who that guy is that you heard in the bathroom, and you're not going to like it," Major Winter said.

Robert waited for the major to continue, but he said nothing, so Robert returned impatiently, "Well?"

"Remember the orbital satellite, the ship that brought those billionaires into orbit, so they could save their own hides? Well, it looks like they are planning something new. They, um, want to force the other comet into orbit."

"What? And how are they planning on doing that?"

"This Mr. Lee is getting paid by the billionaire

known as Mr. Kaser. He is apparently the leader of the billionaires on the Ark."

"Weird," Robert thought, momentarily sidetracked. "You'd think we would have heard of the billionaire leading everything. But anyway, this Mr. Lee is betraying the world for those rich selfish billionaires? And why would they want to put Comet 3 into orbit anyway . . . unless . . . "

"What?"

"Well," Robert said, thinking, "we are hitting the larger comet into a path with the Moon, right? That means that we've essentially ignored the other comet, though according to its current trajectory, it still might hit us. But if what you say is true, then they are trying to redirect the comet to begin *orbiting* Earth. This is very dangerous and very unlikely, because they might accidentally disrupt our plan with Comet 2, by either hitting our missiles, or Comet 2 itself."

"But what would be the advantage of having Comet 3 orbit Earth?"

"Comet 3 has large amounts of elements that are

very rare and very valuable. These billionaires, well, they have a mind for exploiting things, right? So, if the comet were in our orbit, it's possible that eventually we could mine the comet for those elements. But it's very risky, and the orbit would even have to be controlled by us, since the sublimation of the comet would make it unstable."

"Is there anything we can, or should do?" Major Winter asked.

Robert thought about this. "I'm not sure, Earl. I don't know how we can stop them. They have the data, they have resources."

"Does the Ark have missiles?" Major Winter asked.

"I don't think so," Robert replied.

"Do you think that the billionaires could try to get control of our missiles through this Mr. Lee character? If he's planning to use our missiles to get Comet 3 into Earth's orbit instead of guiding Comet 2 to hit the Moon, that would be a disaster."

"I agree, but there's no way they could gain control of the IMPs heading to Comet 2. They must be trying to use future IMPs to control Comet 3." Robert sighed. "I can't believe the billionaires are trying to play God."

"I can," Major Winter opined. "They are selfish, and they want to continue ruling the world, so having a gold mine nearby in space would make sure that they will be the ruling class for millennia, right?"

"Yeah, I guess you're right."

Robert thanked Major Winter for the update and then got back to his own work. There were now only forty-one days until the Moon and the larger comet would collide. Even though Dr. Kang routinely asked Robert for information regarding nuclear bomb-making instructions, he worked well with the man. He did not see Kim Ha Lee frequently as most of the communication was done entirely through Mr. Yuan and Dr. Kang. His nights were spent sleeping either in the government facility at Pyongsong or back at the hotel on the banks of the Taedong River. Robert did notice himself getting skinnier; it seemed the North Korean diet of cold noodles, porridge, and caged chicken lacked more in nutrition than he originally thought.

. . .

Dustin absentmindedly cleaned Esther's lab with Karina. Svalbard was always a cold place, and since the comet impact it had been getting colder. Additionally, the seed vaults were also cooled electrically, as a sort of precautionary measure. He and Karina had worked, with their heads down, for about three weeks. The first week had been hard. Dustin frequently woke up in a cold sweat—the image of Lukas, with a cigarette glowing in his mouth, burned into his mind. Karina woke up like that, too, haunted by her own demons, and neither of them spoke to each other about what had happened. Dustin preferred not to know what happened to Karina. Though Esther had been nice and compassionate toward them after the ordeal, David was not. He'd work them hard, whether that meant cleaning, cleaning, and more cleaning, or cataloguing different chemical and genetic-modification tests conducted by the Malkas.

The Global Seed Vault was a depressing place to work. It was built solely for function over form, and the hallways and rooms had very low ceilings. Fluorescent lights were ubiquitous, and they gave Dustin a permanent, dull headache. The Seed Vault was built into a mountain, so all the space was used—everything was crowded.

Dustin and Karina ate lunch quietly together, or with the Malkas, and Ben was as jubilant as ever. Seeing Ben was always a bright spot in Dustin's day. The only time he was happy was when he was talking or playing soccer with Ben, even though he couldn't kick the ball against the broad side of a barn. "A communist sport" is always what Ben's father called the game, so he never played much.

One day, Dustin was walking along the dark hallway and past the door of the room where he had been tortured, and he stopped. It happened often now; some little thing would remind him of that night, some random table or cigarette or smile, and he would be back, sitting in the dim room with only two chairs and a table, staring at the friendly-faced Lukas. Come to think of it, there were many things about Svalbard that reminded him of that day. In the beginning he and Karina were happy, and they felt lucky that they both had food and clothing and security. But the memories of the torture seemed to grow more terrifying every day and Svalbard was beginning to feel like a prison.

Being at the Svalbard Global Seed Vault gave Dustin knowledge only available to a few people in the entire world: the condition of people on Earth. Though the people at Svalbard were cold and untrusting of outsiders, since the beginning of the comet crisis they had kept tabs on civilizations all around the world. They did this to preserve as much of humanity's culture as they possibly could. Every Monday, a newsletter would be sitting outside Dustin's door, detailing the current state of the world to the best knowledge of the people on Svalbard. It showed a new map of the world, as well, including a black-hole-like area off the coast of France labeled "Impact Site."

He learned the nations in South America were *bunker civilizations (B-civs),* which meant that they were comprised of separate families or communities living in bunkers, and they had no centralized government. The United States was categorized as a *B-civ,* but still communicated with certain regions, including Svalbard—a fact that excited Dustin greatly. It made him wonder about his family, his friends like Jeremy and Anna. Were they still alive? Would there be some way he could find out? Dustin wondered if he would ever return to his home. He wondered if he would ever be free again.

Hegemonic Civilizations (H-Civs) had taken complete control over their people and were the most brutal forms of dictatorships seen on Earth. North Korea fell under this category, as did Russia and a few countries in both the Middle East and Africa. Many of the world's islands had been wiped clean, and island nations like New Zealand fell under the category of *Unknown Entities (UE).* There were no radio signals coming from these places, and no signs of life. This was not to say nations weren't possible *B-civs*, but due to what was known about the impact event, it was unlikely there were survivors.

Lastly, there were *Sovereign Civilizations (S-civs)*, which held power over their people democratically—or at least claimed they did. This included states like China and Norway.

The scientists at Svalbard assumed that there were around two billion people alive on Earth, but this number would rapidly decline because of the critical food shortage, and the farming issues that would grip the world. Some of the scientists jokingly referred to the *B-civs* as Cannibal Countries, which Karina found horrifying, but Dustin shrugged it off. He thought it probably fit.

One day when they were eating in the cafeteria with Esther, David, and Ben, Lukas made an announcement to the room.

"Attention!" a voice from the front of the cafeteria said.

Dustin and Karina looked up and saw that Lukas was preparing to speak. In the three weeks they had been working at Svalbard, neither of them had ever heard Lukas speak. They knew almost nothing about him except that he was one of the leaders of the community on Svalbard. He also smiled at them a lot, which made Dustin and Karina both shudder.

"Attention," Lukas said again, waiting for everyone to be quiet. When the clamor of cafeteria conversation and clanging silverware died down, Lukas spoke.

"I'll keep this short. I know that we at the Svalbard Global Seed Vault value the perpetuation of the human race above all else. There is a very unlikely chance that one of the two comets still headed toward Earth hits Svalbard. Though this has less than a .012 percent chance of happening, we have never been known to rely on odds to get our work done.

"For this reason we have decided to send several shipments of duplicates of our seeds to some trustworthy governments around the world. We want to guarantee that every country that has the capacity to provide for their populations has the *means* to do so as well. Therefore, we are recruiting volunteers to leave 'Santa's workshop,' to become Seed Ambassadors to the world." Lukas chuckled at this nickname of Svalbard, and took in a breath before continuing.

"The simple fact is this: the more area that we can grow food, the more likely humans will survive." As Lukas stopped to take a sip of water, there was a smattering of applause.

"As you know," Lukas continued, "there is a team working on stopping the larger of the two comets from hitting Earth. This is not our objective. Ours is longer-term. We want to work on step two of saving humanity, the food problem." Lukas scanned the room.

"So," he finished, "I'm organizing teams of Ambassadors. All interested persons should talk to me, or Astrid, immediately."

Dustin and Karina eyed each other, both thinking the same thing. Ben noticed the look and asked, "You guys want to leave, right? You want to go back to the United States?"

"Absolutely," Dustin replied, feeling weak with relief.